For Lukas, Dylan, and Julia:
My very own pile of puppies that I love more than anything in the
world.

1

Chapter 1

"I'll do it when I lose the weight," I thought to myself. It was the first thought I had when I woke up in the morning and the last thing I promised myself when I dropped off to sleep. Yet here I was 34-years-old, 5 feet, 11 inches tall, 308 pounds and not doing a damn thing about it. That elusive "it" was to change jobs, get out of debt, be a better mom to Molly and Vinny, a better wife to Andy...just BE better.

"Moooooom!" I was jolted out of my fantasy by the big green eyes and cereal breath of five-year-old Molly pulling the blankets off me. "Mom, you promised we'd walk to school this morning!"

"I'll walk you there, honey," Andy answered before I could say anything. "Mom's got to get ready for work." He was covering for me. He knew that me walking Molly and Vinny to school meant heavy breathing, sweating through my make-up, and pit stains all before 8 AM. He was rescuing me from humiliation and pity-filled stares from the other parents.

The stares were the worst. It must be a regional thing. When Andy and I attended our kids' events at Woodlawn Elementary School in South Fargo, parents and teachers at school would be sickeningly sweet and nice to my face, but I felt their eyes on me after I waddled away from them. I knew they were gossiping about me and how I'd let myself go. It was true. I kept gaining a little more weight each year.

At the school carnival last fall, I'd actually overheard one of the moms say to another, "Do you think Sylvia has a thyroid problem? It's *such* a bad example to set for her kids to get as big as she has. She needs to get control of herself." After I heard this, I hid in the bathroom and cried and texted Andy to bring the kids out to the car so we could leave as I'd made up an excuse I wasn't feeling well. The truth was I had no interest in facing those shallow, bitchy moms. They never talked about anything of substance, just cut people down behind their backs. Moreover, they all had the same stupid haircut. I nicknamed it, "The Fargo Haircut." It essentially looked like a duck butt. I guess the technical term was inverted bob but they all had it. It was like a tattoo so I could tell which women were untrustworthy. I very consciously made sure I kept my hair long so I would never be associated with the duck butt bitches of Fargo.

"I'm sorry, Molly," I said. Great. I'm not even out of bed and I'm already letting people down.

"It's OK, Mom," said Molly. She hung her head and walked out the door of our bedroom.

"I could've done it, Andy," I snapped.

"Jesus," Andy said with a sigh. "I thought I was doing you a favor, Syl." He looked hurt for a moment but that was quickly replaced with defensiveness. "Take her if you want. You'll have to leave in 15 minutes if you want to get her there on time."

He knew I wouldn't be able to do it. At my weight, it took me longer to do everything. I had to take breaks, so I could catch my breath and wipe the sweat from my forehead. And my walking pace is slow because my knees hurt.

Even though it was only a week before Memorial Day, the summer warmth was upon us so there was no chance of me staying cool when I got inside the school with Molly and the other kids and parents. He also knew my self-consciousness triggered my anxiety which made me feel like I couldn't breathe, and then I got dizzy, nauseous, and felt like I was having a heart attack. So not really the scene Molly was looking for at her kindergarten graduation day.

"It's fine," I snarled at him. "You already told her you'd do it."

I heaved myself out of bed and felt every ounce of myself and so, so heavy in my body. My ankles and knees protested on my way to the bathroom and I avoided glancing at myself in the hallway mirror as I passed by. If I didn't look at myself, maybe I could keep my lie going that my life hadn't spiraled out of control in the ways I suspected it had.

Chapter 2

"You can drop me off here, Mom," said Vinny, my eight-year-old, in a quiet voice.

"What? Why?" I asked him, confused, as we were two blocks from his school. First Molly and now Vinny? I was determined to get at least one of my two children to their destination on their last day of school. "Plus there's a busy intersection right here."

"It's OK, I'll cross safely. I'm almost a third grader," he said proudly. I pulled into a strip mall, parked the car, and turned around to look at him.

"Vinny, what is going on?" I demanded. Vinny looked at me. His eyes filled with tears.

"M-m-my f-friends," he stammered, trying to choke back tears. "They call you names." My heart sank.

"What names?" I asked.

"Um, I shouldn't say." He looked ashamed.

"Vinny, it's OK," I encouraged. "You can tell me anything. I'm not going to be mad." He looked up at me with giant brown eyes and took a deep breath before answering.

"They call you hippo, rhino, and elephant, and they say you're so fat you're going to die before I'm a grown-up," he blurted. "Mom, are you going to die before I'm a grown-up?" He was crying full on now.

I turned back around and looked straight ahead out the windshield. Bruno Mars' "Uptown Funk" was playing on the radio and I needed the upbeat pop moment to fill the space between my eldest and me while I collected my thoughts before responding.

"Kids can be really mean, Vinny," I began. "People struggle in all sorts of ways. I struggle with my weight. Some people struggle with drinking too much, or spending too much money, or with their emotions." He nodded and sniffled.

"I think it's easier to be mean to me. You can see my struggle on the outside because it shows in the size of my body." I shifted in my seat as the seatbelt was digging into my hip with my extra flesh pouring out around the safety feature.

"I don't have a crystal ball, buddy," I admitted. "I want with everything in my being to be around for as long as I can. I want to be around when you're a grown-up. Do you think you'll stop picking your nose by then?" Vinny snapped his head up, giggled, and bared his gap-toothed smile.

"I tell them to stop, Mom," Vinny said as we drove the last two blocks to school. "I stick up for you."

"I know, Buddy. Have a great last day of second grade. I'm so proud of you for another great year of learning and growing, and failing and falling, and pulling yourself back up again to rise up and meet the challenges of the day."

Vinny hopped out of the car and I idled there with my sunglasses on, tears streaming down my cheeks. I couldn't promise him I'd be here when he was a grown-up.

Chapter 3

"I'll have the number three," I said into the speaker at the drive-thru after dropping Vinny off. It was my morning routine to get a sausage, egg, and cheese bagel with their special sauce and a side of hash browns and OJ. I knew it wasn't good for me but it made me feel so much better, especially when I had to steel myself for my work day ahead.

I pulled into the park a few blocks from work and devoured my breakfast. I felt disconnected from the entire experience; I just wanted to get to the other side of the meal so I could discard the wrappers where no one could see me. Eating for me is complicated. I despise it yet it fills my thoughts and distracts me most of the day. I hate food and I love food. It's my enemy and my friend.

"Good morning to the one and only, most gorgeous, voluptuous woman in the world, Ms. Sylvia Wilde!" My best friend in the whole world, Roxanne McKay, met me as I badged into the back door of our workplace. Roxanne is a tall, athletic, proud, loud, lesbian black woman and the Head of Creative for Fargo Sporting Goods (FSG). I direct sales and marketing for the women's clothing line and we met 10 years ago when she was finishing college and interning and I had just come on board in the sales department.

Roxy was a track and field star for North Dakota State University (NDSU) until a knee injury sidelined her and dashed her Olympic hopes during her senior year of college. She was in a low place when she came to FSG, and little by little, my sense of humor pulled her out of her shell (along with the medication that also helped pull her out of her deep depression). We've been thick as thieves ever since and this has been our only professional gig since graduating college so we've watched each other grow and succeed.

"Hey Roxy, you svelte gazelle!" I beamed at her. She made me so happy. Her personality was intoxicating. She is so statuesque and recently gotten into ultra-distance running and powerlifting. She looks like an Amazon warrior.

Men are incredibly intimidated by her when she walks into a room, which gives me a deep sense of satisfaction. Her wife Lin is the most diminutive looking Asian woman I've ever seen. She weighs barely ninety pounds, and is not quite five feet tall. She is a chemistry professor at NDSU and is the only person outside of myself that Roxy will take any advice or direction from without putting up a fight.

"How are my Molly and Vinny doing on their last day of school?" Roxy's big brown eyes searched me for stories. Roxy was at both of their births, which made for quite the scene in the delivery room. At Vinny's birth, my midwife, Liz, joked, "I'm not sure who cried louder, your baby, or your friend! She gets a 10 out of 10 on her APGAR score for sure!"

Andy was second fiddle to Roxy in the delivery room as she was my rock through 24 hours of labor with Vinny and 12 hours with Molly. Andy had a weak stomach so he lurked nearby but knew that we women were doing the hard work together to get the babies Earthside. He generally tolerated Roxy but deep down I think he was wary of her and jealous of the connection I have with her.

"They're good! This is going to be one Wilde summer!" Roxy rolled her eyes at me. She was displeased I'd taken Andy's last name when she learned what my maiden name was.

She thought Sylvia Sorenson had such a fun ring to it and she liked to say it in a Fargo accent really drawing out the 'O's' in Sorenson. She's from inner city Chicago and spent a fair amount of time making fun of the Fargo accent. She was in stitches when I pronounced words like "Baaaag" and when I would say "Ope!" when I bumped into someone.

"Good morning, ladies!" I was startled as I heard a cheerful but deep voice from behind me. It was Dominic. Dominic started at FSG at the same time as Roxy and I but was five years older than I was. He directs the sales and marketing of the fitness equipment line and definitely takes care of his body. He's 6'4" and a former Division I basketball standout during his NDSU days. After college, he turned to competing successfully in Ironman triathlons. He's traveled the world competing for the fun and adventure of it all.

He went through a tough divorce four years ago and Roxy and I laugh when we watch the sales associates fall over themselves trying to get his attention.

"Hey, Nic!" I smile. "How many miles did you run last night?"

"Oooh, let me guess," said Roxy. "Ten. No, fifteen!"

"Sixteen," said Nic. I shake my head as Roxy goes on to share her workout adventure of loudly powerlifting in her front yard, while across the street, her elderly neighbors, Ernie and June, made a night of it by pulling out their lawn chairs, sitting on their driveway and watching her put on a show.

"It's time to head into the 9 AM weekly roundup meeting," I said as I held the door into the conference room open for my two lovely friends.

Chapter 4

"Women's, where are we at for sales?" Anna Kasey, the FSG CEO barked in my general direction without looking at me. It was clear to me that she didn't respect me. She'd acquired her role as CEO after her father, Bob, passed away five years ago. We all loved Bob Kasey and he loved us. Anna tolerated us. She would much rather be vacationing in the Maldives with her girlfriends on Daddy's dime as she'd done for many years. She was an only child and her mother died when she was a teenager.

Her father left her the company and a salary, but she had to work in the role of CEO to access it. I'm not sure if she was more pissed at him for not leaving her a fortune with no strings attached, or us for being the motley crew of eclectic Midwesterners she had to put up with on a daily basis.

"Sales are up 30% compared to last year at this time," I shared.

"Bitchin'!" said Roxy with a clap. She then proceeded to do a little victory dance around me despite the blatant discomfort of the other staff and interns as they shifted their eyes, uncertain where to look during the show.

"My notes say we were to grow to 50% more than last year," said Anna flatly, ignoring Roxy's display.

"Ah, um, we talked about that being a lofty goal based on all the competition with online marketplaces and how brick and mortar stores are seeing less revenue," I protested feeling my face flush with anger and embarrassment.

"I want it up to 40% by September and 50% at the end of the year or we will review the women's line at FSG. Do it by any means necessary," she finished.

By her tone, there would be no further discussion about this. How in the hell was I supposed to increase sales in Fargo, North Dakota by 20% by the end of the year? Also, any means necessary? My panic receptors were firing and I felt beads of sweat roll down my temples.

"I gotcha, babe," Roxy piped up, glaring at Anna. "We'll blow Fargo's mind with our campaign!"

"Nothing sexy and no more money for the creative budget, McKay," Anna warned Roxy. Roxy just shrugged, laughed, and continued her victory dance in her chair.

"Dominic, tell me how things are going with the fitness equipment line," Anna purred as she turned her attention toward Nic and flipped her long, blonde hair over her shoulder and leaned in towards him. Her tone was completely different than it had been with Roxy and I and it was pathetic to watch Anna morph into "Helpless Barbie" as Roxy and I nicknamed her when she was in the presence of Nic.

Anna could often be found in the fitness equipment department or Nic's office checking on numbers or asking Nic for advice and insight in decking out her home gym. Anna had been trying before Nic's marriage was over to get her claws in him but had doubled down on her efforts since he became single.

"Not great actually. I lost three local accounts to the national chains," Dominic shared. "We can't meet their price needs because the online retailers and bigger operations are beating us out," he continued.

Dominic went to NDSU for physical therapy and athletic training. He'd worked with everyone from professional athletes to elderly people. He only came to work at FSG at his ex-wife's recommendation. She insisted he make more money to finance cars, vacations, and a lake home. Dominic didn't want those things, he just wanted to help people move well. She had a duck butt haircut.

It was clear that he didn't love the sales aspect of FSG but now with two elementary school kids he got to see every other weekend and a giant child support check, he felt trapped in a job he disliked. I suspected he took a lot of that frustration out on his body as he pounded out the miles on the treadmill and trails, and had an impressive home gym at his residence on the edge of town along the Red River.

"What do you need, Dominic?" Anna implored, with big eyes laser beaming into Nic's. "Just tell me and I can get those resources for you." Roxy and I locked eyes and raised our eyebrows at one another. "Do you need more marketing dollars to move into billboard, or print, or web advertising? Just tell me the number and I'll approve it," Anna peered into his eyes looking for his approval. Nic remained expressionless.

"Thanks," he said gruffly twirling a pen through each of his fingers on his right hand and back again with effortlessness and grace. It gave me such a deep sense of satisfaction that Nic did not give Anna the time of day.

Chapter 5

"How are my grandbabies?" my mother, Kathy, pleaded into the phone. "I can't believe Molly's done with kindergarten! Do you want me to drive up there? What does Vinny need? Is he doing soccer again this summer? Is Andy taking time off so you can go on a proper vaca---"

"Mom, stop!" I couldn't answer one of her questions, much less respond to the full-blown interrogation. "The kids are good and all lined up for their summer activities, camp, and the YMCA day program while Andy and I are at work."

I had to get out ahead of my mother's questions because if I waited too long to call or text back, she assumed we'd all succumbed in a fiery crash on I-94.

"Well are you at least going to bring them to the lake?" My mother had a way of sliding in a little guilt to many of our conversations. It wasn't overt, just enough for me to question how much time I spent at work, and what she thought I should be doing.

I'm lucky, I have a fantastic relationship with my mother, but she stayed home with my brother and I. I think she either resents or downright disagrees with how much I love my work and feel my duties as a wife and mother are second runner-up to my job. I only stayed home for six weeks with each child after their births, and my mother would find ways to support me on my first day back at work with words of encouragement like, "I hope your uterus doesn't fall to the floor," all with a worried look on her face.

She is the opposite of me. She is small-framed and very thin even though she eats whatever she wants. I was bigger than she was by the time I was 11 years old. My dad, Tom, on the other hand, is larger than life in body and spirit. He is tall, broad, and muscular. I got my stature from him. I've always been a daddy's girl and he's always been kind to me. Both he and mom always encouraged me to try all of the sports and extra-curricular activities even if I didn't have a chance in hell of being good at them. I've always been good at volleyball, and they encouraged that. I appreciated they seemed to overlook my size, but looking back, perhaps a visit to a dietician early on could have helped me to not let my weight get so out of control later in life.

"Mom, we'll come to the lake." I hated that I had to remind her that the Interstate ran in both directions and perhaps it would be easier for her and dad to come visit us instead of the other way around. The kids love the lake and they get to hang out with my brother, his wife, and their kids so it makes the hassle of packing up and living in chaos for a few days all worth it to see the cousins together.

"Silas and Katie and the kids will be here over the Fourth of July," Mom hinted. "I would love to have my entire family together over the holiday."

My older brother Silas lives in Minneapolis with his wife Katie and they're both athletic trainers. They met at the University of Minnesota in some sort of bone or muscle class, I forget, and they've been inseparable ever since. They're employed by the University and have chaotic schedules that take them all over the country during the school year with the collegiate sports teams. Their summers are spent vacationing with their two kids, Miles and Hannah, who are the same age as our kids.

"We'll be there for the Fourth, Mom." When I hung up with her, I had a sinking feeling in my gut. Last year, I felt so uncomfortable in my skin. It was punishingly hot and everyone was in shorts, tank tops, and swimsuits, and went tubing and skiing behind the boat. I sat in my chair all day baking under the sun and ordering Andy around to keep an eye on the kids, as I didn't want everyone to see how large my body had gotten. That was when I was 20 pounds less than I am now.

Chapter 6

"What am I going to do? Where do I start? I don't want to live like this but I don't know how to help myself."

"I think you need to start by putting your clothes back on, Sylvia," said my midwife Liz, patting my arm reassuringly. "Then we can make a plan."

It was the first full week of summer and I was having a follow-up appointment after my labs came back from my well woman visit with Liz. It wasn't good.

"You've been getting away with your weight, nutrition, and habits for a long time, Syl," Liz began. "But that's not the case anymore. You have high blood pressure, high cholesterol, you have prediabetes, and your BMI is 43. For your stature, I'd like to see your BMI between 26-28 which would mean your weight would be around 175-185 pounds. I'm worried about you."

I sat on the exam table, defeated. Only the paper blanket covered me from the reality I was facing. Option 1: Do nothing and put myself in an early grave. Option 2: Do anything and start today.

"What should I do first?" I asked Liz.

"Clean up your nutrition," stated Liz. "No more drive-thru. All real food. Track everything. I'm going to refer you to a dietician and I want you to bring her two weeks worth of food journals when you meet with her."

I nodded in agreement. "What else? Should I exercise at the same time?"

"Start with walks. Just to the park and play with the kids. Don't sit and watch from the bench. Get into the sandbox and push them on the swings. Don't sit down. Move once an hour at work. Park in the back of the parking lot at the store. Stop watching TV in the evening," Liz rattled on.

"OK, stop," I insisted. "I'm going to have a panic attack right here if you keep going."

"I helped you bring both your babies into the world, Syl," Liz shared. "Now let me help you stay around long enough to become a grandma."

Chapter 7

"I'm in trouble with my fatness," I said to Andy after the kids had gone to bed. He was watching TV, took a drink of his beer, and didn't look at me.

"Did you hear me?!" I raised my voice.

"Yep." He was clearly uninterested.

It hasn't always been this way with us. We were high school sweethearts. We graduated from a small, rural high school in Haven, Minnesota in 2003. He was on the football team and I was a volleyball star. We were so fit and we couldn't keep our hands off each other back then. We both went to NDSU on sports scholarships and married right out of college. We never worked out again after college and marriage. We were both just so tired. Performing at that level for so many years in high school and college to keep up our scholarship status left us exhausted.

The downside of stopping all that exercise abruptly is that our eating and drinking habits didn't change. The grueling strength and conditioning schedules always left us with the ability to eat whatever we wanted and not gain weight. At my peak performance level in college, I weighed 165 to 175 pounds and was pure muscle yet feminine with exceptional breasts and booty. Andy is 6'2" and weighed 210 back in college. He was solid muscle. Not the same case today. He didn't gain as much weight as I did over the years but he's about 250 to 260 pounds consistently now.

When I look at Andy now, his eyes seem vacant. He's going through the motions of our life together but is completely disengaged from me. He'll interact with the kids and put on a front for them but we've moved to the roommates stage with one another. The moment he gets home from work at 7 PM, he has a 6 pack of beer in one hand and fast food (for himself) in the other. He'll scarf down his food, chat with the kids and play with them until they go to bed at 8 PM. Then he turns on the TV, methodically drinks one beer after another until he's finished the 6-pack and passes out in his recliner around 10:30 PM and I'll hear him get into bed around 1 AM after he wakes up in the chair. When I pressed him on why he doesn't just sleep on the couch instead of disturbing me in the middle of the night, he said, "The children should see that their parents sleep in the same bed."

We haven't had sex in two years. We both got big, and any time he initiates, I shut him down, incredulous that he would want to have sex with me in my shape and condition. I think after so many times being shut down by me, he gave up. He works as a salesperson of farm equipment and he makes decent money but I think we both know it isn't what he was put on Earth to do. He resents that I enjoy my job due to having Roxy and Nic there. I've fantasized about moving on to another job that challenges me in new ways but I don't think anyone would hire me in my physical condition nor would I have the confidence to apply for a new job.

"So are you going to support me in my weight loss and working out journey?" I pressed him further. He shut off the TV and looked at me, tired, and a little glassy-eyed from the beer.

"What's going to be different this time, Syl?" he asked. "I've heard you say this at least five times before. You never stick to your plans. I don't believe you. You start, stop, and gain more weight. I'll believe it when I see it," he finished. Without giving me a chance to respond, he turned the TV back on and cracked open his last beer in the pack.

I stormed out of the living room, and then down the hallway into our bedroom, slammed the door loudly, and flopped onto my bed fully clothed from the workday, contacts in, and make-up on.

26

Tears streamed down my cheeks. He'd given up on me. I was his wife and the mother of his children and he had no confidence in my ability to succeed.

"I'll fucking show him!" I whispered to myself in between quiet sobs before drifting off to sleep.

Chapter 8

"I'd like to start by having you step on the scale," said the dietician, Laura, at our first visit. Fantastic. Let's get the humiliation right out on display, first thing. Time to leap into the abyss of facing reality.

I closed my eyes at first but opened one before she asked me to step off. I caught "302.4" flash across the digital readout before I stepped off. The last two weeks of tracking had already made me feel more accountable to the process and the rage that was building in me to prove Andy wrong steered me away from my morning routine of drive-thru sausage, egg, and cheese bagel and sides. With each of my little wins, I was creating stepping stones that would help me cross this wide expanse to be to the other side where I hoped a healthier me resided.

"Are you active?" asked Laura. I narrowed my eyes at her. I bit my tongue because it was very tempting to get sarcastic and drone on about how many marathons I'd run in the last year.

"No," I admitted.

"Well, based on your weight, you burn 2,100 calories a day just being alive," she said. Was this woman messing with me? "That means, even with light, normal activity throughout the day, showering and getting ready, walking around at work; you likely burn about 2,500 calories."

I was skeptical but listening. I steeled myself to learn I would only be allowed 1,000 calories a day and to plan to be hungry and tortured.

"I reviewed your food logs over the last two weeks," she continued. "Thanks for being honest. I don't see much of that around here." I shrugged. I was not friends with this woman. I was waiting for the other shoe to drop where she handed over her torture and deprivation plan for me.

"It looks like you're averaging around 3,200 calories a day. I think you'll be surprised if you add back in some moderate physical activity, cut out the drive-thru meals, and start eating really simple, basic food. Your body will likely quickly reward you by letting go of the excess weight."

"How quickly can I lose weight?" I asked eagerly. She frowned. "Well, Ms. Wilde, how long did it take you to gain this weight?"

I thought about that for a moment. I had been steadily gaining since I graduated from college and shortly after our wedding. I weighed 175 on our wedding day and I was a little over 300 pounds now.

"Twelve years," I reported. She smiled and sat back in her chair.

"It won't take you that long," she answered. Thank goodness because I don't want to wait until I'm 46 to be at a healthy weight.

"About a pound or two per week on average," she obviously saw me trying to calculate in my head. "Ms. Wilde, this is a messy, non-linear process. To be successful, you'll have to commit to these habit changes for a year or more to reach your goal weight."

She must have noticed the dejected, defeated expression on my face. "This is forever work," she continued. "Some don't have these difficulties. You do. This is the work you'll have to put in day in and day out. It will become more methodical and habitual, but it will always be work. Are you up for the challenge?"

"Absolutely I am."

"Fantastic, let me help draw up a three-month healthy meal plan for you."

Chapter 9

"What in the hell is this, Syl?" My mother yelled from the kitchen. I sauntered in from the living room into the kitchen to see what she was talking about. "I told you to bring potato salad!"

"It's wild rice, broccoli, grapes, and sunflower seed salad tossed in a little light vanilla yogurt," I answered her cheerily. The beginnings of the afternoon/evening fireworks could be heard at the beach. My mother stared blankly back at me. "Why? Where is your famous potato salad?" She seemed so small to me. She had more than enough in terms of personality to make up for her small stature.

"I'm working on cleaning up my diet, Mom," I shared. "This is really hard for me so will you please be supportive?" I heard Molly's happy shriek and looked out the window towards the beach where my brother Silas had lit a firework that created a giant plumage of pink smoke.

"So now you can't have potato salad on the Fourth of July?" Mom asked incredulously. "I don't know what kind of doctor you're seeing in the big city, but it isn't right to cut out food. Food is joy and celebration!" she said exasperated.

"OK, first of all, I've met with a dietician, so I'm not working with a shady doctor or on weird drugs or shakes to lose weight," I felt the need to defend myself. My mother can be skeptical of our life in the "big" city of Fargo. She and my dad come only for the necessary things like cheaper groceries and specialty medical appointments. The allure of urban life is completely lost on them. They can't sleep if it isn't completely still and quiet. The times they've stayed with us overnight, they wake up constantly due to sirens, train horns, and the garbage truck.

"Mom, my life is changing in a big way, so I hope you can be on board," I continued. She looked at me with concern in her eyes.

"I just don't want you to be let down again,' she said sorrowfully. "You've done so many things over the years to try to lose the weight, and none of it has worked or stuck. I worry that you're just setting yourself up for disappointment." I felt heat rise into my cheeks and my anger triggered.

"Thanks for your support, Mom," I said sarcastically. I turned and walked out of the house down to the beach to be with my children where they were joyfully bounding around the fireworks area with their Uncle Silas and their cousins Hannah and Miles.

Time to add my mom to the list of people that have zero confidence in my ability to succeed.

Chapter 10

"How has the last month been, Sylvia?" asked my dietician, Laura, at my one-month follow-up visit. "What have your challenges and successes been?"

"Can I stop you right there, Laura?" I asked. "It's going to drive me crazy if I don't know how my food choices and tracking have been going if I don't know what's going on with my current weight. Can I weigh in first?"

"No," Laura responded kindly but firmly. I was shocked. Not many grown-ups say 'No' to me and I wasn't sure what my next step should be.

"Why?"

"If you're complying with the program, your weight will be down from our last visit. There's no way to hide from behaviors that derail you because the scale will tell the story," Laura responded confidently. "Now, tell me how the last month has been, Sylvia."

I shifted in my seat as I reset my expectations for this check-in with her. I went on to tell her how my husband and mother did not support me and how disappointing that was to me. I shared how alone I felt in this process. I continued with how the first week, I broke out in a flop sweat and racing heart when I drove by my breakfast drive-thru spot. Even following a specific meal plan, and not even being hungry, I'd felt despair as if I were breaking up with a comfortable but lazy boyfriend that only wanted to have sex but never wanted to take me out on a date in public.

"Believe it or not, my kids have been the most supportive," I said as I shook my head. My five and eight-year-old children would ask me if they could bring me my pre-made, portioned meals I'd prepared, or if they could fill up my water bottle for me. Vinny even asked if he could ride his bike slowly next to me one night when I headed out into the late July heat for my daily 45-minute walk.

"What about your husband?" Laura pressed. I snorted. I had to decide how honest I needed to be with her about Andy.

"He's ignoring what I'm doing," I stated. "He hasn't changed his behavior at all. He still eats fast food every night, drinks too much beer, and doesn't offer to pick up any of the fresh fruits, vegetables, or do any of the meal prep with me."

"How does that make you feel?" asked Laura with alarm in her eyes.

"Honestly, I feel stronger and more emboldened to continue on," I answered. Any moment Andy went out of his way to be unhelpful or sabotage my efforts, I unhooked from the transaction with him and disengaged. I could tell he was getting frustrated but there was something brewing inside me that just didn't care. I had been with this man ever since he was a boy when we started dating in high school, and I no longer felt it was my job to make sure that my life wasn't inconveniencing him. So often in the past, I'd give up on things I do for me because I didn't want to ask for too much help from Andy. No longer.

"Are you ready to step on the scale?" Laura asked when I finished my recap.

I did the same routine as last month where I closed both eyes when I got on and when asked to step off, opened one to glance. The digital readout flashed 289.4 pounds. Thirteen pounds down since last month! I was doing well and good luck to anyone that got in my way and tried to stop me.

Chapter 11

"Lower!" Roxy screamed. She was coaching me through a grueling late summer strength and conditioning workout in her front yard. As sweat rolled off my forehead, face, and chest on to the mat underneath me, I heard a holler from across the street.

"You can do it, you're almost done!" said Ernie, the elderly neighbor who made it a habit to watch Roxy's front yard workouts. I smiled and shook my head at the craziness of it all. His wife, June, was walking across the street carrying a tray of ice water with lemon.

"Five more, Sylly girl, you've got this," Roxy was inches from my face as I finished my push-ups on my knees. After I finished my set, I collapsed in sweet victory and shaky exhaustion.

I'd asked Roxy to light a fire under me to exercise and she took this request very seriously. In addition to her work as a creative master at FSG, and her own ambitious training goals, she also trained clients from time to time. She was very picky. She wasn't interested in working with people who didn't want to put in the hard work it was going to take to make progress. She absolutely would not work with people who were slacking off in the kitchen. When I first told her I was going to meet with a dietician and lose weight and asked her to train me, she said 'No.'

"Why not?" I asked, shocked.

"Because you eat like shit," she said matter of factly. I thought about being offended and giving her the cold shoulder but I appreciated her honesty.

"What if I follow the dietician's meal plan to a T so I don't blow it in the kitchen after I work with you? Will you take me on as a personal training client then?" I proposed.

"Yes, but you have to pay," she stated. "One hundred dollars per one hour session, once per week, and I'll give you a strength and cardio and rest and stretch plan for the rest of the days when we're not meeting."

"OK, but why are you charging me your regular training rate? Can't I get the friends and family discount?" I countered.

"Absolutely not," Roxy said. OK, now I was starting to get pissed she was playing such hardball with me. Didn't she want me to succeed?

"I need you to have skin in the game. You'll sign a contract with me for one year, I'll take the first and last month's fee up front and I'll take the entire fee whether or not you quit on me."

My mouth dropped open. "You really want to take $4,800 from me over the next year?" I could not figure her out.

She just shrugged. "It's actually $5,000 as you'll be using my home gym equipment so there's a $200 usage fee. Take it or leave it." She extended her hand to me to shake on it.

I didn't need to think about it. I was absolutely taking it. Roxy was just one more person to whom I would prove my grit and resilience. I shook her hand.

Chapter 12

"How was your Labor Day, Sylvia?" Laura asked as I sat across from her for my two-month check-in for my weight loss plan.

"It was good," I shared. "I think my mom is starting to catch on that I'm no longer going to bring my famous potato salad to our family functions at the lake." I chuckled remembering back to the week prior. My mother scowled as she peered into the bowl of my broccoli and wild rice grape concoction, which was my new potluck staple to share.

"Well, Sylvia, it looks like you've lost weight," my mom observed. "I can tell in your face. Your cheekbones are more prominent and your jawline is more defined." I smiled.

"Thanks, Mom!" I reached out my arms to hug her. "Want to sneak in a quick walk and talk with me before this holiday celebration gets too crazy?" She beamed at me and linked arms as we headed out the door to walk the lake loop. The hilly three-mile adventure gave us the opportunity to greet the neighbors and watch them remove docks and pack up their lake homes in a long goodbye to summer. It was a hot, sweaty, enjoyable walk with Mom, which I cherished because she and I hadn't been out together walking and chatting for years. My mother is absolutely delightful and filled with stories. She's funnier than I remembered which made me realize where I get my sense of humor and ability to tell stories well.

"How has it been for you to attend these family functions and stick with your meal plan goals?" Laura continued. I thought for a moment about the difference between the Fourth of July with family and this more recent Labor Day celebration and recounted the many work-related picnics, invitations to grill-out with neighbors and friends, or attend happy hours for appetizers and drinks.

"At first, it was anxiety producing," I began. "Then it became more and more easy. I had my elevator speech planned as to what I was going to say when offered food or beverage I didn't want to have or didn't serve my desire to reach my goals."

Most people I encountered had been respectful of this but some rudely pressed me about why I couldn't "live a little" or that one night out of drinking and junk food wouldn't kill me. As I got stronger and more confident in my resolve, these little jabs began to bug me. I realized quickly which of my friends and co-workers were supportive and which were downright saboteurs.

I could always rely on Roxy and Nic to be supportive at work, but any time Anna attended these functions, she always had a way of working in an indirect jab aimed at cutting me down. Our company picnic in mid-August was a prime example.

"Sylvia, can I get you a burger or a hot dog?" Anna asked from the serving line.

"No thanks, I'll pass," I declined. "I had a lovely grilled chicken salad before I came and I have my eye on all these fruit and veggie sides." Her eyes narrowed at me.

"It's all in the mind, Sylvia," she replied. "If you have a strong mind and are disciplined from the beginning, you will never have these control problems you're having."

Control problems? What the hell? I don't know what she thought she was trying to teach me or if she assumed she was imparting great knowledge but she was usually my least favorite part of my work day. I didn't get it. She seemed to have it out for me. Did she despise my fatness? Was she jealous of my close friendships with Roxy and Nic at work? Whatever the case, she seemed hell-bent on being unsupportive of me personally and professionally.

"Well, whatever the case, what I'm doing is working as I've already lost 13 pounds," I replied, maybe a little too loudly and upbeat. I wasn't going to let her ruin my night by cutting me down.

"Are you ready to weigh-in today?" Laura asked.

"Absolutely." I was excited to learn my number. I even kept my eyes open the whole time. The digital read-out on the scale flashed 278.3. I was down another 12 pounds, bringing me to 25 pounds lost since I started with Laura on nutrition and Roxy on exercise. I was working the plan and the plan was working!

Chapter 13

"Mommy, I can fit my arms around you now more than before," Molly looked up at me with big green excited eyes. "Before I could only hug your front and now I can hug your front and back!" I was leaning over to hug her as I dropped her off at her fall gymnastics series. My child had so much energy I had to help her channel it to the good. The weather had turned cooler, but I had just dialed in more into my training plan and Ms. Roxy Ultra marathoner had convinced me to run/walk a 5k in late October.

"Thanks, honey!" I said excitedly. I didn't even look around me to see if the other parents noticed Molly's observation. If they did, they know now that there is less of me. I watched her bound out on the sprung floor without a care in the world, totally within her body and happy in its ability to carry her through her days. I hope she never loses that raw confidence in herself.

"Well hello there," said a voice behind me. "Nic!" I said excitedly. "What are you doing here?" I wondered, looking around trying to figure out why he was also at gymnastics drop-off.

"Sammy's trying new things." At that moment, Nic's seven-year-old daughter peeked from behind her towering dad. She had obviously been crying. She certainly didn't seem very interested in trying this new thing. I took one look at her and knew what would help.

"Hi, Sammy! I'm Sylvia," I kneeled down to get to Sammy's level. She responded by burying her head in her dad's shirt. "Would you like a friend to stay with you during your first night at gymnastics?" I asked. She responded by shaking her head 'Yes' still not showing her face.

"Molly," I called out over the gymnastics floor. She saw me and came bounding back toward where I was standing with Nic and Sammy.

"What is it, Mommy?" she asked excitedly. "I have a very special task for you tonight," I told her, and her eyes lit up in anticipation.

"I need you to be very special close friends with Sammy tonight," I said. Sammy peeked out just one eye to look at Molly. Molly marched straight toward Sammy.

"C'mon, Sammy," Molly said, grabbing Sammy's hand and pulling her away from her dad. "You have to stay with me so I can show you the balance beam, uneven bars, and the bouncy floor and trampoline. If you're really good, you can run the runway and jump into the foam pit." Sammy just nodded and held on to Molly's hand as they marched back toward the group. She looked back at her dad once and he smiled, waved, and gave a thumbs up.

"Wow, she's quite the ringleader," Nic said, laughing. "I thought this would be a total fail. Thank you so much Syl, for getting her out there. How old is Molly now?"

"She's six. Just started first grade," I said and added, "I've only been called to the principal's office once this year. She can be very passionate about things she cares about."

"The apple doesn't fall far from the tree," Nic said. I felt my stomach do a little flip. "When you care about something, you double down, Syl." Well, he was right about that!

"So what does a gymnastic parent do for the next two hours?" a bewildered Nic asked, looking around the large quonset building with tons of kid shouts, coaching, and loud music.

"I'm going on a walk!" I said. "I can catch up on all my favorite podcasts. I actually might do a little interval work as Ms. Roxy has me signed up to do the 5k this fall." Nic's eyes lit up.

"Oooh, do you mind if I come with you?" Nic asked excitedly. Ha! How would that go? I would be going at a crawl pace based on what he was used to in his training.

"Are you sure you want to?" I challenged. "Aren't you running a marathon this fall?"

"Yes, but today is my rest day," he said. I raised my eyebrows. "Come on Syl, I can't be trapped in this metal building for the next two hours with these child screams and loud pop music."

For the next two hours, Nic and I proceeded to walk, run, talk, and laugh through the tree-lined streets of South Fargo amidst the beautiful changing colors of the leaves and the warmth with just a bite of fall cool in the air. I learned about how the last few years had been going for him after the divorce, how his kids were adjusting, and I shared how I'd committed to a journey of better eating and exercise.

"I'm so proud of you, Syl," Nic said. "This is tough work you're doing day in and day out. I bet Andy is proud of the hard work you're putting in every day." I snorted.

"He hasn't said a word, Nic," I admitted. "He has not said *one* word about the food choices or how I'm exercising more or how

48

I've lost 40 pounds for Christ's sake!" I felt my cheeks flush and it wasn't from exerting myself. "You didn't realize you'd be joining me on rage cardio, did you Nic?" I flashed him a smile that he returned.

"I'm happy to be here with you, Syl," he said genuinely. "Same time next week?"

"Absolutely! The gymnastics time will fly by!" I agreed.

We walked back into Fargo Gymnastics Club to find Molly and Sammy sitting cross-legged across from each other, braiding each other's hair giggling and laughing. They popped up when they saw us walk in.

"We're best friends, Mommy," said Molly excitedly. "And Sammy is so good at gymnastics." Sammy nodded and stood up taller with pride. This was not the same child I met two hours ago.

"Can I have a playdate with Molly?" continued Sammy. "We have to get better at gymnastics so one day we can join the competitive team like the older girls that wear make-up!"

"We'll see," said Nic looking at me with a smile. We all walked out together in the crisp fall air.

Chapter 14

"How did your 5k go last week?" asked Laura excitedly. It was now the first week of November and I was doing well. There was a Halloween themed run that the Fargo Runners Club puts on every year and it was so much fun to be at a race participating with Nic and Roxy instead of cheering them on from the sidelines as I had in years past.

"It was so amazing," I swooned. "I think I'm really athletic and strong underneath all of this." I made a sweeping gesture from the top of my body on down to my toes.

"I definitely know that to be true, Sylvia," Laura agreed. "I'm so excited to watch you move through this, marrying your nutrition and exercise programs together. Sometimes it's such a battle to convince people to move their bodies well and fuel their bodies well. You get it. I can see that you're motivated." I smiled at her and nodded in agreement.

I had moved on from being afraid of the scale and the dreaded news it would reveal to me. I was now encouraged to learn what my progress would be month to month. I was five months in and had a six-month follow-up appointment with my midwife Liz to check my bloodwork and blood pressure to see if I'd made a change in how my body was functioning. The weigh-in with Laura at the end of our session revealed that I'd dropped a total of 45 pounds in five months bringing me down to 257 pounds.

"Now, Sylvia, I want to warn you that your initial weight loss has been somewhat rapid," Laura began. "You're losing on average 2.25 pounds per week. You might start to see plateaus and weeks where you maintain instead of lose," Laura warned me with a serious expression. I smiled at her reassuringly.

"You know, I don't even mind," I said honestly. "This has been so much more about the process and the journey than it is about the end goal and I have enjoyed every step along the way." I practically skipped out of her office.

On my drive back to work, I remembered the week before when my children watched me cross the finish line of my first Fargo Halloween 5k. My mom and dad brought Molly and Vinny to the race and they were dressed up in their Halloween costumes.

Molly was Dorothy from *The Wizard of Oz* and Vinny was Spiderman. They held up signs, and cheered their support. I'll never forget the look of pride on their faces and even watching my mom and dad beam with pride at my accomplishment. I may not have run fast, but I jogged the whole time without walking once. I finished in just under 40 minutes and it was the most enjoyable public spectacle I'd had the opportunity in which to willingly participate.

I had a smile plastered on my face the entire time. It was delightful to look at all the costumes around me, the families running together, the older runners, the elite runners, all coming together in our community to celebrate one another. They had so many activities going on for kids and families after the race that I opted to stay and play with the kids in downtown Fargo and wait for Nic and Roxy to cross the finish line as they were both running in the full marathon.

I started running at 8 AM so I was done before 9 and Nic would likely finish around 10:30 AM and Roxy around 11:30 AM as their marathon started at 7 AM. The kids and I got breakfast together in downtown Fargo at the famous Mom & Pop diner, Bison Breakfast Bar. We said goodbye to my mom and dad and headed back to the finish line in time to welcome Nic across the finish line.

We learned that he finished in the top ten in his age group and it was quite the scene to see him in all his glory; tall, slender yet muscular, a set and determined look in his eyes as he crossed the finish line.

"Nic! That was amazing!" I said as he came through the finisher's chute drinking chocolate milk and eating a banana. When he saw the kids and me, his eyes lit up.

"Thank you!" Nic said, excitedly, sweat pouring off him. "It hurt a little bit the last five miles but it was all mindset at that point. I knew my body could do it. I needed to convince my brain that we were almost done," he smiled victoriously. He looked around.

"Where's Andy?" Nic asked. My smile faded.

"He's watching football and day drinking at the bar," I said flatly. Nic frowned and looked down at his watch.

"But this is your first 5k! And it's only 10:30 in the morning," Nic said, exasperated. I threw an arm each around Molly and Vinny.

"My mom and dad were here and I have my cheer squad right here with me!" I said giving the kids an extra squeeze toward me. "Where are Sammy and Ethan?" I said changing the subject. Molly's ears perked up when she heard me say Sammy's name.

"They're with their mom this weekend," Nic said sadly. "Sarah wouldn't switch weekends with me so they could watch me." Nic perked up, suddenly with an idea. "*You* can be my cheer squad!" Molly and Vinny heard this and began shaking their noisemakers. Nic loved it.

"Should we go wait for Roxy to cross the finish line?" I asked.

"Yes," Nic said. "I have to keep walking and stretching and eating food or I will be incredibly sore and locked up tomorrow." Our crew headed back toward the finish line to be the ultimate cheer squad for Roxy. It was a good thing because we almost missed her grand finish.

"Put your hands together for Roxanne McKay, ladies and gentlemen!" the announcer said as Roxy came rocketing toward the finish line. We all cheered and screamed along with Roxy's wife, Lin, who we'd found at the finish line spectator area. In true Roxy fashion, she'd run the marathon in full Wonder Woman regalia.

A tall, strong, powerful black woman dressed as Wonder Woman was one of the most powerful things I've ever seen. I was so proud to be Roxy's friend and that she was with me on this journey to be a better version of myself. I felt tears of love and pride welling up in my eyes for my dear friend. Roxy held up the widely recognized Wonder Woman "crossed arms" in front of her body and literally roared across the finish line. The crowd erupted in cheers.

Chapter 15

"Do you make anything else these days?" My mother raised her eyes at me when she saw me put my wild rice, grapes, and broccoli salad in the fridge. I had to jockey for space in her refrigerator because of all the sides and dishes waiting to be served.

"Mom, are there more people coming to this party that I don't know about?" I asked looking at the food volume. It looked as if she had enough to feed 30 people. In addition, that excluded the turkey my dad was smoking outside and the mashed potatoes my mom was currently whipping up on the stove.

"I feed my family, Sylvia," my Mom said. "That's how I show them I love them," she said honestly. Huh. Well at least she's honest about it. She's a feeder. She'll make her family so fat that they can't run away from her. I thought I'd probably need to unpack this concept at a later time in a therapy setting. The holidays were not the best time to work through years' worth of enabling, codependent behavior patterns in my family of origin.

"Mommy, come watch the parade with me!" Molly ran toward me, arms outstretched. It was tradition for us to watch the Macy's Thanksgiving Parade on TV. I looked at my mother for her approval to join Molly as I typically helped her set out the food spread (along with consuming nearly a day's worth of calories in snacking and finger licking bowls and spoons).

"Go ahead, girls," Mom said. "Don't come crying to me if one of those large balloons carries a small child into the clouds like Mary Poppins, separating her from her parents to go live in the sky," Mom warned. Molly giggled and ran over to hug her funny Gramma.

Dad, Andy, and Vinny were already watching the parade festivities on TV. I smiled as I stood behind the scene, letting the warmth of family and gratitude envelop me. My enjoyment of the moment was interrupted by the audible crack of Andy opening a can of beer. I looked to the side table next to where he was sitting. There were two empty cans already. My Dad glanced at Andy and then his eyes met mine with concern. I shook my head and shrugged.

It was obvious to me that the more I focused on my self-care and wellness the last half of a year, his drinking escalated. He was becoming more untethered and I found myself creating more distance from him. I'd typically try for one bid for engagement a day with him but was invariably met with anger or despondency. I didn't push it further and moved on with my day, habits, and routines.

Several years ago I suggested he go to talk therapy, or change jobs, or hang out with friends more, or pick up a hobby, or see a doctor about getting on antidepressants. This did not go over well. He was angry with me and I coped by eating more food. My mindset was so different now. His self-destructive tendencies were difficult to watch, but I'd decided that if he wasn't going to let me in to help or share in the burden, I had to release myself of the responsibility of his actions.

The only time I saw a spark in his eyes was when he was playing catch with Vinny. The sessions were getting shorter due to Andy getting short of breath and wanting to sit, drink, and watch TV. He also loved cheering on Molly on as she zoomed her bike up and down the block. He was also her judge, scoring her on her backyard gymnastics routines (10/10 always).

"Want to go for a walk?" I snapped back to attention. My brother Silas appeared.

"Oh, Brother!" I said and threw my arms around him. They had just gotten in from the Twin Cities and Hannah and Miles were already hugging hello and doing goofy happy dances with Molly and

Vinny, emulating the dancers and shenanigans they were watching on TV.

"Can I come, too?" Katie popped her head from behind Silas. "After the drive, I want to stretch my legs and move a bit before the big meal." I looked to my dad for approval.

"Go ahead, darling," my dad said cheerily. "Andy and I will hold down the fort with the kids because your mom will just shoo us away if we try to enter her domain while she's creating her masterpiece up there." That was a very accurate observation. I looked over at Andy and he had drifted off to sleep and was snoring. I'd wondered if he'd had a few beers this morning before we left based on him being passed out by 11 AM.

Silas, Katie and I headed out for the lake loop that included hills, beautiful lake views, and delicious conversation with my beloved brother and lovely sister-in-law. It felt so good to be able to keep up with the walk and the conversation with them. I remembered years gone by when I'd resent them for their spontaneous holiday walks.

I knew I couldn't participate because my knees would hurt, I'd slow them down, I'd be huffing and puffing and red cheeked, and would sweat soak through my clothes even though the weather was crisp and cool. As we rounded the final corner to walk down the hill to rejoin the family for the Thanksgiving meal, I thanked my body for not giving up on me, and giving me this chance to honor it and thank it by moving well and nourishing it well. I had so many more things to do with my children, family, and friends. I needed a strong body to carry me through all my days.

Chapter 16

"Look, Sylvia!" Roxy called out to me. "I'm black, lesbian Santa Claus!" Roxy did a twirl for me with her very tight Santa suit with thermal layers for warmth underneath as we lined up for the Running of the Reindeer 10k near the Red River that divided Minnesota and North Dakota on a chilly December Saturday a few weeks before Christmas. I had opted for my regular running gear and had merely added a Santa hat for good measure. If there were a costume contest component to this race, Roxy would have certainly won it.

My weight loss and wellness journey continued to clip along successfully and I hadn't felt this good and energized and happy in years. My six-month follow-up with Liz, my midwife, had gone well, too.

"Oh my God, Sylvia," Liz said as she entered the exam room. "I just read the rooming nurse's notes and it says you've dropped 70 pounds since you last saw me in July. You weigh 232 pounds, your blood pressure is almost within the normal range, and your labs you did this morning came back much lower for fasting blood glucose and cholesterol. What on EARTH have you been doing?"

I spent a moment letting her pride in my ability to turn my situation around wash over me.

"Well, you scared me pretty badly when you said I was a walking medical crisis about to occur at any moment," I shared.

"After that, the rage motivation kicked in," I added. I went on to share that Andy hadn't been supportive or confident in my ability to change my eating and exercise habits nor had he shown any interest in improving himself.

"Who is supporting you, Sylvia?" Liz asked, concerned.

"I have a tribe," I said. "It's small, but it's mighty. Roxy, my best friend, is also training me and has gotten me into running and lifting weights. My friend Nic has been supportive by not making comments about my progress one way or the other. He hasn't treated me any differently than when I was bigger and more unhealthy. My kids are fabulous. They're the best motivators I could ever ask for." I thought for a moment. "But it's mostly me."

"What do you mean? Just you?" Liz asked, confused.

I went on to explain to Liz that after all I'd been through over the last decade of gaining weight and slipping into poorer and poorer habits, I had no one to blame but myself. There was no one forcing me to make the choices I had. Nothing, not my own health, or getting pregnant twice and having two kids, had offered enough of an incentive or a foothold for me to climb back out of the hole I dug for myself. Luckily, I realized that no one was coming to rescue me. I had to rescue and care for me. That was exactly what I intended to do.

"Well, it sounds like you're doing all the right things. Keep up the great work!" Liz was beside herself with the progress I made which was fine but I truly didn't require it to feel validated in my path. "I won't need to see you again until next July for your annual well woman exam. I certainly don't need to prescribe anything to help you manage. I still have you taking your antidepressant. Do you want to continue taking that?"

"Absolutely," I said quickly. "I'm not Wonder Woman. I have moments of weakness and I tend to run a little anxious and overfocus on things so it helps me stay nice and level so I can accomplish these things."

Liz smiled. "Please don't fire me as your provider," she joked. "You've got your life figured out and you're managing your life better than I am!"

As I returned my mental focus to the race, I looked up to see the mile five sign for the Reindeer Run. I glanced down at my watch. I was holding a 10:00 minute mile pace. This was unbelievable! I blinked my eyes a few times, as my eyelashes were frozen. (Frozen lashes are a rite of passage for Fargo runners. Frozen beards are a sight to see as well.) I wondered if I could finish my first 10k in a time of one hour even. I did some quick calculations in my head and landed on trying to get progressively faster over the next mile and a quarter.

Exactly 50 minutes had elapsed at the five-mile mark. I went within my body and noticed as the pace ticked down to a 9:30 minute mile pace for the first quarter mile. I leaned my body forward, pushed myself to get 9:00 minute mile pace, and held that for the next quarter mile. I was so determined I couldn't quit now. My lungs burned and my legs were starting to feel like Jell-O.

I swallowed and pushed into an 8:45 minute mile pace for a quarter mile and then an 8:30 minute mile pace for the final quarter mile that led me into mile six. At this point, I looked ahead of me and about 100 yards away I spotted Roxy's fabulous self. I had to try

64

to catch her. I started to sprint and caught up with her. We only had about a tenth of a mile left and we both looked at each other.

We're both competitive women. We were in a stride-by-stride foot race to the finish line and cheers of support roared in our direction. It took everything I had and I felt like I was floating above the ground. We were so close! As I was five strides to the finish line, I leaned my entire body forward so far I thought I might topple over.

I crossed the finish line a hair ahead of Roxy. I met my goal of finishing my first 10k in under an hour and achieved an unexpected, where-did-that-come-from-behind win over Roxy. We stood at the finish line and cried, and hugged, and froze. She pushed my shoulders back so she could look me square in the eyes.

"I knew you were in there, Syl," Roxy said crying and smiling. "I knew you were made for so much more." I hugged her back and let my tears flow. This was a huge step in redeeming myself and living life in the body I was meant to inhabit.

Chapter 17

"Is Daddy breathing, Vinny?" I asked worriedly.

"Yes," Vinny responded, his voice shaky. "He just won't wake up. He snores every once in a while and, um, I think he peed his pants, Mom."

"You and Molly hang tight and I'll be there shortly, OK?"

Unbelievable. It was two days after Christmas and I had just returned to work after the holiday. Andy took extra time off work to stay home with the kids as they were on break from school. He had promised them a few days of ice skating, sledding, and snowman building. They were so pumped. It was only 11 AM and I assume Andy started drinking as soon as I left for work that morning at seven.

"Roxy, can you update Anna in the meeting at 1 PM on my department sales for the year?" I had burst into her office and thrust a stack of my numbers for the women's clothing line sales in Roxy's hands.

"Of course, but what's going on?" Roxy asked alarmed. I explained that Vinny had just called letting me know that Daddy wasn't waking up and had pissed himself. Roxy's eyes narrowed and she crossed her arms. She was incredibly protective of me and always wary of Andy and his lack of ambition to improve himself in any way since she'd known him.

"You've got to be done with this, Syl," she said. "This is becoming a safety issue for the kids. He's sick and needs help. What if he had gotten in the car with the kids and then blacked out?" Roxy threw up her hands in disbelief of the hypothetical catastrophe. "I'm coming with you."

"No, absolutely not," I said sternly. "I have to deal with this on my own." I felt a hard lump rise in my throat and threaten to cause me to cry in frustration and anger but I swallowed hard. "I need you to keep Anna off my back until I can figure out my game plan today." Roxy hugged me tightly and I eventually pulled away from her embrace and rushed out into the frigid, punishing Fargo winter wind to try to attempt to save my children from the trauma of witnessing their alcoholic father go off the deep end.

Chapter 18

"Andy, wake up!" I shouted in Andy's face when I got home. I told the kids to go down to the basement and watch a movie while I helped get Daddy awake and cleaned up.

"Is he going to be OK?" Vinny asked with big, scared eyes, lower lip trembling, trying to hold back fear tears. Molly was holding his hand and her raggedy stuffed elephant that I hadn't seen in a few years in the crook of her arm, sucking her thumb which I also hadn't witnessed her do in ages. Shit, they're already traumatized. I didn't rescue my babies in time to save them from this scene.

"He is sick," I said. "He needs help and I have to get him to a place where he can get some help." I gathered them both up in a mama bear hug and shooed them away to the basement for their movie.

After shouting and shaking Andy for what felt like an eternity, he suddenly lurched upright in our bed and threw up all down the front of my dress and my shoes. He looked up at me, grabbed onto my forearms for support and weakly said, "Help me,

Syl," his vomit plus whiskey breath and profuse sweating forced me to breathe through my mouth as I was feeling nauseated.

"Get in the shower, Andy, and we'll take it from there," I said flatly. I helped him out of his urine, vomit, and sweat soaked clothes and stripped off my dress and shoes and changed into my winter sweat suit. I tore the blankets, sheets and pillows off the bed. I rolled everything up into a giant snowball of shame, disappointment, and resentment, and walked outside and deposited the giant thing into the garbage can.

The torn wrapping paper and new toy packaging from just a few days before in the garbage can was in sickly stark contrast of a throwback to a simpler time than what I had to steel myself to deal with now. There was no amount of detergent or scrubbing that could undo this low point Andy and I had reached in our marriage.

When I got back inside, I could still hear the shower running. I pulled out my cell phone, touched "Cameron" in my contacts, and placed the call.

"Hello? Syl?" Cameron answered, likely bewildered as to why I would be calling him. Cam was Andy's football buddy he met our first year in college. Those two could drink anyone under the table and since Cam didn't have a girlfriend at the time, Andy, Cam and I spent a lot of time together. It was obvious early on that Cam had a schoolboy crush on me but I never played into it as I was deeply loyal to Andy.

Cam went on to meet the sweetest music major our senior year and they married a few years after us. They'd decided as a couple not to have children and spent a lot of their downtime traveling and adventuring together earlier in their marriage. His wife Eleanor teaches music lessons to kids and adults when she's not traveling extensively as she is a concert pianist so her job takes her to New York and Los Angeles for weeks at a time.

Cam works as the Director of the Fargo Parks District, a job that suits him well as he wants everyone to get outside, no matter the season and get involved in the community whether they're young or old.

"I have a favor to ask you," I said mustering up the courage to be direct, assertive, and ask for exactly what I needed right now.

"Anything," Cam said. I knew he meant it.

"I need Andy to stay with you for the next month," I said, my hands starting to shake with the realization of what I was doing to

70

our family unit. "His drinking problem has gotten out of hand, and it's not safe for him to be around the kids right now."

"Damn it, Andy!" Cam responded. "Did he hurt you, Syl? Or the kids?"

"No, no," I said. "He's never been physically abusive with me or the kids. He's self-destructing, Cam. He needs professional help. Can you please come get him this afternoon? He's been drinking and I think he'll be a little sobered up by the time you get here."

"I'll be there within the hour," Cam said.

"Thank you, Cam," I said genuinely as I felt my adrenaline levels go down and I started to feel more within myself and in control.

Andy stumbled into the kitchen with fresh clothes on and sat down at the kitchen table. He began to cry. My caregiving instinct was to go to him and hug him and let him know things would be alright but I held my ground as I knew if I got too emotional, I wouldn't be able to carry through with what I had to do.

"Andy, Cam will be here to pick you up by three," I said, glancing at the clock, which showed 2:08 PM. "You'll be staying with him for a month." Andy opened up his mouth to respond and I held up a stop sign hand. His shoulders slumped.

"It is your choice what you do next, I will not pressure you either way," I continued. "If you quit drinking completely, and see your doctor for a checkup and start taking antidepressants and enter talk therapy, we may be able to salvage our marriage and keep our family together." I said feeling the confidence rise within me. "If you do not, we are done. What you're doing to yourself is unsafe and the children and I don't deserve to bear witness to your self-destruction."

Andy nodded. "I'm going to go apologize to the kids and say goodbye," he said rising from the table. He paused and turned around to face me, unsteadily, as the whiskey was still coursing through his system. "You're stronger than me, Syl, you always have been."

I slid down to the floor as he left the room and buried my face in my hands. I was sure I'd just torn apart our family and booted out my partner which didn't say much about my commitment to the "In Sickness and in Health" portion of our wedding vows.

I had no idea if what I was doing was heartless. I kicked my husband out of the house on one of the coldest days of the year. I didn't have much time to wallow in my indecision as I heard a light knock at the front door.

"Hi Cam," I said. I knew I looked like hell. My mascara had run down my cheeks and I'm certain even though I'd changed clothes I still reeked of Andy's whiskey vomit.

Cam drew me up in a deep, warm hug that felt so reassuring. I realized that I hadn't been shown affection from a male in so long that I found myself holding onto to his strong, powerful frame trying to siphon off enough strength and power as I could. I knew I'd need it to sustain me in the coming month.

"Wow," Cam said his voice low and gentle as he stood back and looked me up and down. "You look so incredible, Sylvia." I hadn't seen him in over a year and he was likely shocked by the 80 pound weight loss since we'd last seen one another.

"Thanks," I said. I meant it. My appearance was the last thing on my mind but I was so grateful for Cam being here at a time I needed him most.

"Hey, man," Andy walked to the doorway and greeted Cam. "It appears I've spun out of control," Andy said as he held on to a wall for support.

"Let's get you good again so you can keep your family together," Cam said matter-of-factly.

As they drove away into the cold December afternoon, I knew nothing about our marriage and family would ever be quite the same again.

Chapter 19

"Sylvia, I'm going to have you talk to Karen," my father-in-law said gruffly. Kenny Wilde wasn't known for his warmth. A retired farmer from North Dakota, love was shown to his children through changing their oil and helping them buy their first cars. When it came to the touchy feely stuff, Karen Wilde, my mother-in-law, took the lead.

"Sylvia?" Karen asked, worry thick in her voice. "What's wrong? Are you OK? Andy and the kids? Has there been an accident? The weather's been terribly cold!" My mother-in-law tended to run anxious and when she was worked up, it was hard to get a word in edgewise.

"The kids and I are fine, Karen, it's about Andy's drinking problem," I cut in before she could speculate wildly and catastrophize about wintry car wrecks.

"Oh, I know he likes to have a drink or two now and then but I can't imagine it's too bad," Karen said cheerily.

Ignorance is bliss. She hadn't realized or failed to recognize the severity of Andy's drinking habits and how they'd steadily gotten worse and more problematic over the years. Problems were usually swept under the rug in Andy's childhood as he grew up in the small town of Dooley, where it was important for his farming family to keep up an outward appearance of happiness and success.

When Andy's older sister Carrie had been killed the summer before her senior year of high school after driving drunk and smashing her car into a tree, Andy and his family moved to Haven, Minnesota where his family had a lake home. They kept the farm in Dooley.

They just couldn't bring themselves to face the shame of the choice their beautiful, brilliant, and athletic all-star daughter with a full-ride softball scholarship to the University of Minnesota the following year had made. When I met Andy our sophomore year of high school, Carrie had only been gone a few months and it was painful to be at the Wilde house.

Andy and I ended up spending more and more time together, me playing volleyball and him playing football incredibly well, and he never said more than a few words about Carrie, usually around the time of her birthday. Sometimes I pressed him about Carrie, what she was like, what they did together as children, but he never revealed anything.

He always changed the subject and said, "She's dead now, so what's the point of talking about her." It was always incredibly sad to me but I felt I needed to respect his space and not press him on the issue.

His father was a verbally abusive alcoholic when Carrie and Andy were in their youth. He sobered up when the kids were in junior high when Karen threatened to leave him. Kenny knew that a divorce would look terrible in the eyes of the townspeople of Dooley and being a third generation farmer. He wasn't about to give that tradition up (or half of everything to Karen in a divorce). As soon as we graduated in 2003, Karen and Kenny left Haven, returned to Dooley, and never really discussed Carrie again.

"Karen, this is serious," I said sternly. This was the second time today I had to muster up all my emotional strength and courage to say the tough things that needed to be said aloud and ask for help.

"Andy was blackout drunk today while watching the kids and urinated himself and threw up on me when I finally roused him."

There was silence on the other end of the line.

"Andy is staying with Cameron here in Fargo for the next month and hopefully he will make the right decision to get help to get sober so we can keep our family together."

"What can I do, Sylvia?" Karen said quietly, sniffing. I could tell that she was crying.

"I need you and Kenny to come stay with the kids until they return to school after the New Year," I said directly. "My parents left yesterday to spend January and February in Colorado, so I need you to help me."

My heart was pounding in my chest. Karen and Kenny were so excited when Vinny was born and spent a lot of time with us. When Molly was born, they recoiled from us. As Molly and her personality grew, it was clear to me that Molly reminded them of Carrie.

Molly was the spitting image of her Aunt Carrie. It became more and more difficult for them to spend time with her as it brought up too many painful memories.

There was a long pause on the other end of the line. I thought about bailing on my request and trying to figure out another arrangement. I stopped myself. I had to remind myself that I wasn't being an inconvenience. This was an opportunity for Karen and Kenny to help me at a time of great need. I'd never asked anything so large of them in the nearly two decades I'd known them.

"Yes," Karen said, barely audible. I could tell she was choking back more tears.

"When do you need us to be there?"

I took a deep breath. "Tomorrow," I said, knowing it was a three-hour drive in winter weather conditions from Dooley to Fargo.

"The babysitter can stay until noon tomorrow," I said. Courtney, our lanky swimmer babysitter, had been our summer nanny the last three years but as her high school years were coming to a close, I needed to cast my caregiver net wider to make sure I could keep good and proper care for my children.

"We'll be there," Karen said. "Will you be at work until five?" Karen asked cheerily.

I was certain that we weren't going to go into great detail about the ins and outs of my husband's addiction, and the unresolved trauma from his childhood surrounding his father's alcoholism, and his sister's untimely death also associated with alcohol.

"I'll make sure you have a warm meal when you get home," I felt my shoulders rise up a bit with this burden lifted, knowing they'd be here for the next week helping me keep my head above water and helping me take care of the children.

Chapter 20

"I don't know if I can approve this," Anna said flatly. I was meeting with her to request some time off the last week in February to fly with the kids to visit my parents in Colorado. Andy was working toward sobriety, started AA, and began an antidepressant. However, he'd had two incidents in the last month where he'd faltered and began drinking again. Cameron and I had been in touch a few times a week over the last month and he'd said that he'd made strides but was still very much so in the early stages of recovery. Cameron was a good fit as a mentor for Andy as he'd been sober for eight years. He and Eleanor both had strong genetic links to alcoholism and addictive tendencies in their families so decided that they would not have alcohol as a part of their life together.

"Why not?" I responded, feeling myself getting flustered. "I've given you a month notice." Why was Anna trying to wreck my plans? I needed to get away from the shit show that was my marriage and I didn't even care that I was going to another wintry place in winter.

"It's a week before the launch of the spring line and I need you here to put out any fires if they come up," Anna responded.

"I have a plan in place with the creative department and my assistant," I argued. I had all of the directives in place and they'd already been handed off to Roxy and my assistant Heather who were more than capable of handling any problems that arose in my absence.

"I'll think about it," Anna said, unconvinced. "I'll let you know at the end of the day."

I pushed back from the desk, stood abruptly, and took an extra moment staring down at her, silently fuming. There were so many things I wanted to yell at her for being an unfeeling, uncompassionate boss. She looked up at me.

"Is there anything else?" Anna asked, annoyed.

"No," I said my heart pounding wildly with rage. As I walked out, I was so mad at myself for not speaking my mind and saying more. She knew what I was going through with Andy. I returned to work late the next day and was honest and open with Anna about what was going on in my personal life with Andy's alcoholism and treatment plan.

I let her know that I would do my best at work but asked for a little space and grace as we adjusted to what our days looked like.

She'd looked at me directly after I'd poured out how my life as I knew it was shattering apart and said, "Any unplanned time off will be marked in your permanent record. We can't make any exceptions for leaders."

After that exchange with her, my heart broke a little about my job. I loved working with Roxy and Nic but it was becoming less appealing to pretend that I could do meaningful work under Anna's toxic leadership. It certainly didn't seem like the right time to start looking for jobs when my husband was taking an extended leave from work to receive treatment for alcoholism. I was trapped in a job I'd outgrown and becoming a victim of life circumstances beyond my control.

"Step into my office, please," Roxy stepped out of her office as I was charging down the hallway after my most recent demoralizing meeting with Anna. I bee lined into her office, collapsed on her couch, and began to weep.

"I can't do this anymore," I wailed. "I am so fried. My in-laws are here and emotionally constipated about their own trauma, the kids are confused, sad and scared, and I'm being treated like a child at work."

Roxy pulled up a chair and bore witness to my emotional breakdown. She was quiet, calm, and kept feeding me tissues and water. I released like a waterfall. I complained that I thought that if I took better care of myself, I would be equipped to handle anything that came my way but I was failing. My marriage was failing, my job was failing, and my ability to do anything about it was failing.

"Aren't you going to say anything?" I snapped at Roxy. She was quiet for a moment.

"I'm letting you finish because this is all the wailing you get," Roxy said. I turned my puffy eyes to look at her.

"What the hell is that supposed to mean?" I sure hoped that Roxy wasn't bailing on me now too, but with my track record lately, it wouldn't surprise me.

"I will not stand for your desperation," she said. "No one is coming to rescue you, Syl. This is the hard work that no one else is capable of doing. Andy has been treating you like shit for years. Anna hasn't respected you and she's treated you poorly since she became our boss."

My mouth dropped open. Roxy is usually honest with me but these things hurt.

"So the question is...," Roxy continued. "When will *you* not stand for your desperation? *You* are the one that saves *you*."

It became extremely quiet and all we heard was the light hum of the customers moving about the store a floor below, the soft classical music station playing in the background. I took a deep, shaky breath, and brought myself back to a seated position.

"How do I look?" I asked Roxy. I knew my mascara was running, my hair was a mess, my nose was running, my cheeks were red, and my eyes were almost puffed shut.

"Beautiful," Roxy said, and she meant it.

I left Roxy's office, walked down the hall to Anna's office, and pushed open the door. She was meeting with Nic. She was seated on the end of her desk in a very short skirt and high-heeled feet dangling off. Nic seemed to be relieved to see me. His expression quickly turned to concern.

"Syl, are you OK?" Nic hopped up and came to me. "What happened?" I held up a stop sign hand to Nic. Anna looked annoyed that I was interrupting her day yet again with my problems.

"Anna, I'm taking the rest of the day off," I said, voice shaking. "I will be taking the time off in February to visit my parents in Colorado. I have worked here for 10 years, I have the time, I have made plans for the time I'm away, and I will go. If you have a problem with this, we can discuss my separation agreement, severance package, and my HR complaint placed against you."

Anna's eyes were huge and a flash of fear crossed her face. Nic was looking at the ground but I saw a distinct grin at the corner of his mouth.

Chapter 21

Valentine's Day wasn't typically a big celebration day for me but since having kids, we made it a big deal to have heart shaped pancakes and red construction paper hearts adorning our home. My eyes flew open to the sounds of Molly running down the hall toward my room. I glanced at my smartwatch, which read 5:06 AM. Here we go!

"Mommy!" Molly catapulted onto my bed. "Happy Valentine's Day! I love you so much!" This child warms my heart. Even through the changes of the last six weeks with Andy being out of the house and her time with her grandparents, she remained resilient and celebratory of the little things. I hope she never loses this incredible spark.

"I love you so much, darling," I said gathering her into a tight mama bear hug. "We better get started on our pancakes!" As Molly and I headed down the hallway, Karen poked her head out of the guest bedroom.

"Good morning, Syl," Karen said with her hair poking out in every direction. This made me smile. Karen was usually so put together. It was enjoyable to watch her formal appearance layers peel back a bit during her and Kenny's extended stay with us.

"I know you like to get your morning workout in before the kids get up." I had become close with Karen and she was supportive of my routine of exercise and never made me feel bad when I declined some of her decadent dinner creations. I was so appreciative of her and Kenny's help with keeping our lives from spinning more deeply into chaos.

"Grammy!" Molly ran into Karen's arms. "Will you make the pancakes with me this year?" Karen wrapped her arms around Molly.

"Of course, Angel," Karen said. "You better get Grampy up too so he can learn how your Valentine's Day traditions go around here." Molly bounded into the guest room and jumped on Kenny and the room exploded into giggles and tickles.

Karen had taken to calling Molly "Angel" and it seemed to be very healing for her. She was able to love and appreciate Molly instead of being sorrowful for the loss of her own daughter. I'm certain Molly had no idea she looked so much like her Aunt Carrie, she just felt like a queen to be called "Angel."

"Thank you, Karen," I reached in to give her a big hug. "I'm so grateful for your and Kenny's support. There is no way the kids and I could be getting through this well without you. You two being here makes all the difference."

Karen's eyes got bright and welled with tears. She sniffed and quickly blinked them away.

"Off you go," Karen said quickly.

Well, it was progress. Karen wasn't completely ready to let down her guard but she was slowly warming. I headed back to my room to change into my workout gear. It was a running and lifting day and based on the heavy snow falling outside and the -40 degree wind chill, I decided that it would be a treadmill run and barbell/plates workout.

I smiled as I started my warm-up. This treadmill has been in my possession for five years but never used. Nic got me a great wholesale deal from FSG. It served as a clothesline until this winter. I loved getting sweaty, doing interval sprint workouts, long runs, and steep incline work which I had done more of lately in preparation for my trip to Colorado.

I was pumped to hike around in the mountains and maybe even go skiing. I couldn't wait to spend time with my parents and show the kids the mountains. My parents were staying in Steamboat Springs, so I also hoped the mountain passes weren't closed and we had clear driving weather.

It also just so happened that the week we were going to be in Steamboat, Nic was going to be there for the annual fitness expo that he attended each year to check what was the latest and greatest in fitness equipment and gear for FSG. We'd already planned to meet up and go for a mountain hike or run or maybe a trip to the hot springs.

I was a little nervous about the hot springs part as I hadn't gone swimsuit shopping in years. I had no idea where to start. It vexed me so much that Roxy and I planned a quick weekend girl's trip to Minneapolis to get two or three perfect suits. I hadn't been out of Fargo in so long that it was a grand adventure I looked forward to with my best friend.

As I returned to the kitchen after a sweaty workout, shower, and having gotten ready for work, I found Grammy and Molly dancing in the kitchen. Vinny was carefully flipping the heart-shaped bright red pancakes on the griddle.

"Mom!" Vinny said, and flashed a huge smile at me. "I made this one just for you!"

Vinny handed me a plate-sized pancake. There were raspberries lining the outside of the heart with two small sausage patties for eyes in the center and blueberries arranged below that in the shape of a smile.

"I know how important it is for you to have fruit and protein for breakfast and I didn't put any butter or syrup on yours."

This strong, sensitive child was so observant and so caring about those around him. He'd always been fiercely protective of me but I'd seen him struggle after his dad went out of the house. He was trying to figure out who to be mad at and who to be loyal to through it all.

Some days he was very distant from me and other days he was cuddly and close. I didn't push him one way or the other, just let him move through what he was feeling, always available to him to talk through the big feelings.

"Thank you, buddy," I said, accepting the plate and bowing a bit in gratitude to him.

"That was so thoughtful of you and you're showing me how much you care about me by noticing the things that make your momma thrive!"

Vinny beamed and hugged me tightly. Just then, the side door off the kitchen flew open and Kenny stepped in, bringing winter with him.

"You've got a clear path out of the driveway, Syl," Kenny said, cheeks red from cold and exertion.

"You better get going soon though or the snow will fill right back in the space I cleared! Are you sure they won't let you work from home?"

I smiled. Kenny definitely showed his love for us through taking care of handyman things inside and outside the house. He also loved spending time with the grandkids and was just a big softie under his stoic farmer exterior. I knew not to hug him. However, the kids and I were wearing him down. He would roughhouse with the kids and recently let Molly climb up in his lap so he could read her a story.

"Thanks, Kenny, I appreciate you taking care of us." Kenny nodded approvingly.

I sat down, had a lovely Valentine's Day breakfast, and then packed up the kids and their gear to drop them off at school with their giant homemade valentine boxes. As I waved goodbye from the school drop-off zone, my phone buzzed with a new text notification. I looked down and felt my stomach flip. It was from Andy. It read:

Happy Valentine's Day, love. I'd like to take you out for dinner.

Meet at 7 PM at our favorite Indian restaurant?

I heard a honk behind me to keep the drop-off lane moving. I texted back "Yes."

Chapter 22

I arrived at the Indian restaurant at ten after seven. The weather was horrific, windy, and snowy so it took awhile getting there. When I got in the door, I started scanning for Andy. I was nervous and flustered and I didn't know what to expect from this dinner.

My emotions were all over the place. I didn't see him at first and then started to feel pissed off thinking that he stood me up. Then I saw him. He waved from our favorite corner booth in the back. The one we frequented in college and the early years of marriage. While all our friends were eating at chain restaurants, Andy always wanted to go deeper and explore the fun restaurants in town we didn't have access to in our youth and I loved that about him.

I swallowed and strode toward our booth. I hadn't seen him in a little over six weeks. He stood up as I approached, arms outstretched. I hesitantly went in for the hug he offered. It was so odd to have him show any semblance of affection toward me. I didn't trust the hug.

"Oh Syl, you look so amazing," Andy said into my ear as he held me.

I felt myself get a little weak in the knees. I hadn't had sex with Andy in two and a half years closing in on three this spring and I felt the slightest bit turned on. He smelled so good and familiar. He didn't smell of alcohol and there was a spark that had returned to his eyes.

"You look good, too," I said quietly. "Have you been working out?" He went on to explain that living with Cameron for the last six weeks meant eating like he did and behaving like him.

That meant 5 AM wake-ups, working out for an hour in his home gym together, clean eating and preparing for the day's meals ahead. It also meant reading books, no TV, and finishing the day with journaling and meditation. Andy had dropped 25 pounds over the last six weeks.

"Wow, Andy, that's really great," I said. I was so proud of the progress he was making on his own. "Can I ask you a question?"

"Sure, anything babe," Andy said sweetly. Another stomach flip. I steeled myself from feeling anything as a protective mechanism. The familiarity and sweetness that he was showing me was testing my ability to stay focused about some things I needed to ask and clarify.

"What have you learned about yourself since being sober?"

He nodded and took a sip of his water. I noticed his biceps rippling out of his red polo shirt and had to blink back to make sure I was making eye contact with him.

"It's all the hard work I've put off because I didn't think I had to do it," he admitted. "We were coasting, Syl. The kids are healthy and beautiful, you have a job you love and friends you enjoy, and what do I have? Years worth of unresolved trauma from Carrie's death that I never dealt with, and my parents certainly didn't encourage me or show me a path to healing. It's like she never existed and they tried to erase her. Alcohol helped to ease the pain that started to eat me alive. The guilt of being the *one* alive child in my family, the terror of waiting for the other shoe to drop, like one of my family members getting hurt or dying. I felt like I deserved all of this pain. That it was my cross to bear to be a part of the living. Are you OK?"

My mouth dropped open and I realized I was holding my water glass midair and I hadn't taken a drink. I was paralyzed with the shock of the words that were spilling out of my husband's mouth. He had been in so much pain for the entirety of our time together and never let me in to shoulder the burden of this heaviness he was carrying. Tears sprung to my eyes. I blinked them back, took a drink of my water over the growing lump in my throat and set my water glass down.

"Uh, yes, I am. Go on, Andy. This is just a lot to take in at once," I said, naming my discomfort but allowing the space for him to continue.

"I had a few slips in the first three weeks in January. I've been sober now for three weeks," Andy said with a smile.

"Syl, I'm so sorry," Andy said, reaching his hand across the table to hold on to mine. The lump in my throat had grown to a point where I felt I could barely breathe.

"My road is going to be a long one. I've got a lifetime of work to undo old habits and find ways to replace the bad habits with good ones."

He took a deep breath and I could tell he was nervous.

"I'd like to have another chance with you and the kids," he said. "Can I come home next month and we can take it day by day together this time? I want to support you and make up for lost time."

Before I could answer, the server arrived at our table.

"Can I start you two lovebirds off with some garlic naan bread with hummus?" she asked cheerily. The room started to spin. I stood up from the table quickly. My water glass spilled and tears started falling uncontrollably.

"I'm sorry, I can't stay," I mumbled to Andy and the server. I hurried out of the restaurant into the snowstorm. The wind and snow pelting my face gave me relief from some of the pain I was feeling.

Chapter 23

I spun my tires back and forth in the snowbank about 10 blocks from the Indian restaurant. The blizzard had picked up and the street I had turned onto near the river was blown in with snow. I wasn't going anywhere. I was panicking. Who should I call? Who would be out on a night like this? I looked up and realized I recognized this part of town.

"Hello? Syl?" Nic picked up the phone on the first ring.

"Hey, Nic, I'm so sorry to bother you tonight," I said sniffing back tears trying to get ahold of myself. "I'm sure you're busy and I jus---"

"Oh no, I'm just winding down for the night," he said. "Sarah has the kids this week so I'm flying solo." I worked up the courage to ask for the help I needed.

"Can you help me, please? I'm at the end of Woodland Lane and I got my car stuck in a snowbank," I admitted sheepishly.

"Syl, put your flashers on so I can see where you are and hang tight," Nic sprang into action. "I have the plow attachment on the front of my truck already so I will come get you. We'll let Fargo

99

Police know your car is stuck there and you can come back for it when the snow clears." I was so relieved. "One more thing…"

"What?" I asked, eager to be of help in a situation that was beyond my control.

"You're going to have to stay with me tonight," Nic said. "Is someone staying with your kids?" Oh God, the kids! I told Nic I'd call my in-laws and let them know. We hung up. I called Karen and Kenny and let them know that I was OK, that Andy and I hadn't gotten through our meal but had made progress, that Andy was doing really well on his sobriety journey, and that I wouldn't be coming home. I went on to explain how I'd gotten my car stuck and a friend was picking me up and I'd see them tomorrow, and, finally, to please send my love to the kids.

Then, I texted Andy and said that I was so proud of his progress and didn't expect to learn of all the things he'd revealed tonight. It was a lot to take in and I needed time to process it all. He texted back that he understood and he was willing to take all the time I needed to feel good about the direction things were headed with us and our family. It was such a stark contrast from the last time I'd seen him, when he was at rock bottom. I texted back, "I love you and this has been the oddest Valentine's Day ever!"

I saw a truck headed my way, plowing a path. Nic hopped out of his truck and walked over to the car, holding up a hand to shield his face from the wind and snow. I grabbed my purse, turned off the car, and hopped out. I had been so distracted before I left, I hadn't dressed for the deteriorating weather conditions. I looked down to see my flats sink directly into the snow as I shrieked from the shock of the cold snow on my feet.

"I'm going to pick you up now and you're just going to have to be OK with it," Nic said, turning around. He bent over and looked over his shoulder at me. "Hop on, Ms. Wilde." As if this night couldn't get any weirder, now my co-worker and strong, tall friend was going to haul my body out of a snowbank. I put my hands on his shoulders and felt the muscles underneath my hands even through his heavy winter coat. I hopped on and he confidently hooked his forearms under my knees and walked the both of us out of the snowbank. He placed me down gently at the passenger side of his truck as if he'd done this multiple times before.

When we were both in the truck, he paused to look at me before driving us back to his house. "Syl, are you OK? What are you doing out here?" I quickly flipped down his visor and opened the lid that revealed a small lit mirror. To my dismay, my mascara had streaked down my face, my hair was matted to my forehead from my hat, and my eyes were puffy and red from crying. I quickly closed the visor and turned to face Nic. "I met with Andy tonight for dinner," I began, feeling embarrassment and confusion rise within me about what had transpired over the last hour. "I hadn't seen him in six weeks and he's working on his sobriety and it's going well," I paused to look at Nic to see if this was too much personal information for him. We usually stuck to lighter, brighter, more enjoyable topics like exercise, Roxy's antics, our ideas on fitness trends and equipment, and our training journeys. Nic seemed unfazed by what I was sharing and even looked sympathetic. "Nic, we didn't make it 10 minutes before I panicked and left the restaurant," I felt my stomach grumble. "We didn't even get to order! I'm hungry." Nic turned back to face front and maneuvered the truck down Woodland Lane toward his house.

"Well, we've got some work to do to redeem your evening in that case, Syl," he said brightly. "You can shower if you'd like to warm up. I'll make you my famous cilantro lime chicken and rice, and then we can wind down with some yoga because you need a little more calm in your life," Nic said confidently. I didn't argue with anything he recommended. It sounded divine.

When we got back to Nic's I was instantly comfortable in his space. It was a beautiful, modest home, with simple style and function. Minimal furniture, high ceilings, lots of soft lighting, and big picture windows overlooking the Red River. He had over an acre of land which he'd told me filled with birds, deer, and other forest and river creatures in all the seasons.

"I'll leave you some sweatpants, t-shirt, and a sweatshirt and wool socks in the bathroom upstairs with fresh towels," Nic said, eager to be a good host.

"Thank you, Nic," I said, so grateful for his hospitality as I had no way of anticipating my evening would end at Fargo's most wanted bachelor's house on Valentine's Day in a snowstorm. I headed upstairs to shower as I was starting to feel a bone-chilling cold settle in from when I stepped directly into the snowbank. I stripped off my black leggings, red belted tunic, long pearl necklace, and pearl stud earrings. I turned on the shower all the way hot and let the steam heat fill the room. I saw a scale in the corner of the bathroom and realized that I had no idea where I was on my weight loss journey. It had taken a back seat to the rest of the chaos that had come up in my life. I was very fortunate that I'd dialed in my exercise and nutrition routines so I didn't really have to think about it.

I hopped on the scale to see where I was at, and it flashed, "212." Huh, it turns out that I'd dropped nearly 80 pounds in eight months. I swiped the steam off the mirror to look at myself. I could see the definition in my arms and in the top of my abs. The lower part of my stomach was flabby and my belly button was hiding. I smiled. I spent a moment thanking my body for the hard work it had done taking care of me and vowed to continue to take care of it.

I stepped into the shower and let the near scalding water wash away my cold and lighten the burden of my confusion about how to respond to Andy's request to come home. If I was being honest with myself, my initial gut reaction was, "No." I wasn't ready to let him back in when he was so early in his recovery. On the other hand, I felt so guilty about keeping Andy and his children separated for too long. I had no right to prevent him from seeing Molly and Vinny. I resolved to call Andy tomorrow and make plans for him to spend time with the kids at our house the weekend before we went to see my parents in Colorado. I finally turned off the hot shower after 20 minutes of pure bliss. I smelled like men's shampoo, conditioner and body wash but was clean and warm so I didn't care.

My stomach grumbled as I made my way back downstairs to the kitchen. Nic scooped a portion of cilantro lime chicken and rice on my plate and added a spinach salad with strawberries and apples tossed in vinaigrette on the side. "Red wine or LaCroix?" Nic asked.

"LaCroix," I said. I hadn't had any alcohol since Christmas and it was serving me well. I liked being clear-headed and I slept better and recovered better from long workouts.

Nic and I ate at the kitchen island. I was so hungry that I am certain I wasn't minding my manners. I was so hungry and the food was so delicious, I devoured my food. Nic laughed and said, "You have quite an appetite, Syl!" He turned back to the stovetop. "Do you want seconds? I have more of everything."

"No thank you, Nic," I said feeling full and satisfied. "I usually take more time to savor my food but tonight has been *unusual*." He glanced at my outfit. "Nice sweat suit!" I looked down at my trendy athleisure gear Nic had dug out for me. "Thanks for this, too, Nic," I said gesturing from my head to toes. "You take your time finishing your food, Nic," I continued. "Do you mind if I check out your gym in the basement and get ready for our yoga session?" Nic smiled. "Go right ahead, Syl."

When I entered his gym, I was astounded. It was divided into four corners of activity with an open space in the center to move freely and all four corners of the room had floor to ceiling mirrors. In one corner was an Olympic lifting area with barbells, plates, and collars set up surrounding a squat cage and bench in one corner. Along another wall was a dumbbell, kettlebell, and medicine ball rack with a few more benches to put in work.

The opposite wall held a variety of cardio machines including a rower, ski erg, assault bike, air runner, and treadmill. Finally there was a wall with a ballet bar and section of wood floor for more aerobics and yoga based work and there was a bin of yoga mats, foam rollers, and resistance bands for recovery and strength,

106

balance and flexibility. It was an absolutely beautiful set-up and clearly Nic had put in time and consideration into the design of this room. He came in at that moment as I was taking it all in and feeling proud of my friend.

"What do you think?" Nic asked. "There's also a rolling door if I want to incorporate some outdoor work or sprints as the back of my property opens up to the Red River trail system."

"I think it's absolutely phenomenal," I said. "Check this out," he said with a remote in his hand. All of a sudden, the bright overhead lights switched to soft lighting and tonal yoga music began playing. "You've thought of everything!" I said, delighted. "Oh, I can play some pretty righteous metal music from the 80s when that's the mood I'm in," he said. "Let's get to work on relaxing," he said as he pulled out two yoga mats and bolsters for us. "Would you like to do a yin yoga session and finish with a long savasana?" He asked.

I was impressed that he knew what both of these things were. Yin yoga was completely silent and each of the poses and stretches were held from one to three minutes. It can feel brutal in body and mind.

"Absolutely after a day like today," I agreed.

Nic fired up one of the basement's TVs and cued up a yoga session to stream. I closed my eyes at the beginning of the session and let the session instructor guide me through the movements. The only things heard over the next 45 minutes were Nic and my breathing patterns, the tonal yoga music, and the instructor's calm voice. By the time I found my final resting position in savasana, I was nearly sleeping. I melted into the floor, putty in the hands of the instructor telling me to "Let. Go." I felt Nic's fingers brush mine at the end of the savasana. I didn't pull my hand away. I slipped my hand underneath his and he held my hand.

Maybe it was my deep state of relaxation, but I felt pleasure and safety from his touch. I didn't feel uncertainty, it just felt right. As the instructor invited us to rise to a seated position, Nic and I released hands and followed the instruction. As we slowly blinked open our eyes, I looked over at Nic. He had a serene expression on his face and his blue eyes sparkled in the low light of the room.

"Nic, that was amazing," I said softly. "Thank you for being exactly what I need right now." I paused. "Can I confess something to you?" He nodded at me.

"There is nothing I would love more than to have the night of my life with you by making love to you and surrendering to whatever you'd like to do to me," I said looking him directly in the eyes. "Oh, Syl, I'd love to do that, too," he admitted. "I've had such a thing for you for so long. I didn't know what to do with it because I was married, and then divorced, and you're married, and it's never been the right time to be honest with you about this."

"Nic, I have no idea what to do with this," I said honestly. "I've felt it too under the surface but I haven't always been a confident woman and I would second-guess what I was feeling even though my gut was telling me there's chemistry between us."

"What are we supposed to do?" Nic asked.

"Sleep with me," I said. He raised his eyebrows at me. "I need you to hold me in your arms and feel your strength around me. Our lives are both very complicated and we have kids so we have to be careful with each other." Nic agreed.

"Well, in that case, would you like to come upstairs and go to sleep with me?" Nic asked, hopefully.

"Absolutely, Mr. Bennett," I said. We held hands and walked up to his bedroom and peeled back the down blanket and crawled into bed. He wrapped his arms around me and I got to be the little spoon. It felt so good and I drifted off to a restful sleep, the wind howling outside as the storm raged on.

Chapter 24

"Mommy, it's a snow day!" Molly shouted into the phone. I had slipped out of Nic's room early in the morning to sneak back into his basement gym. "Oh Molly, that's so much fun!" I said matching her excitement. I'd returned to my yoga mat from the night before and planned to do a little light stretching and warm-up and then move to cardio and lift some free weights.

"Sweetie, I got my car stuck in a snowbank after my visit with Daddy and I got to have a surprise sleepover at my friend Nic's house because of the storm. I'll be home later today after the plows come through and I can get my car out of the snowbank," I said.

Molly squealed, "Mommy did you get to see Sammy?" Nic's daughter Sammy and Molly had become quite close during the fall gymnastics classes they took together and now they were re-enrolled in the winter session together. Even though Sammy was a little older than Molly, they got along famously.

"No, I didn't honey. She's staying at her mom's house with her brother Ethan." Molly was OK with this because she said she'd be jealous if I got to have a sleepover with Sammy and she didn't.

Molly and I hung up and I got down to business with my workout. I was half-way through my round of sprint intervals on the rower when Nic appeared in the doorway in his workout gear.

"Man, I have to get up pretty early in the morning to beat Ms. Wilde to the gym," Nic said and flashed a smile at me. His hair was a little wild and bed-headed and it made him look even more handsome. "Try to keep up, Nic!" I said as I resumed another rowing sprint. "You can join me if you'd like. I'm doing intervals on the rower for four minutes, then I lift legs, rower, arms, rower, abs, and I'm going to finish with a burpee ladder."

When I get going on my workout, there isn't much that will slow me down and I couldn't miss the opportunity to play with Nic's fun workout toys. Nic jogged over to where I was, grabbed a remote from a shelf behind me, cranked up some epic 80s rock tunes and we proceeded to work and get sweaty over the course of the next hour. I led Nic in the workout, guiding him through what we were doing next. I had been watching the time on my watch, but when Nic realized the cadence of the work I was doing, he fired up the interval wall clock.

We worked together well and it was so easy to be with him in this space. We were encouraging of one another throughout the workout and at least for now, we didn't have to deal with the elephant in the room that was revealed last night regarding our feelings for one another. For the time being, we had the delightful flow of friendship.

As we collapsed sweaty on the floor after our last burpee on the descending burpee ladder, Nic grabbed the remote and changed the music to something a bit more calming for us to stretch and cool-down to on our yoga mats.

"Well, Nic, I'm going to have to ask you for another shower, another meal, and another set of clothing." He laughed. "My pleasure, Syl. What do you usually eat for breakfast? I was thinking of making myself a spinach and tomato basil three egg omelet. Can I make one for you, too?"

After the workout we just had? "Absolutely, yes!" I said. "And please add a side of toast for me because I assume we'll have to do some shoveling and snow blowing to even make it out of here to go get my car at the end of the lane?" Nic nodded and we spent a few more minutes relaxing and shooting the breeze before motivating up to breakfast.

"Listen, Nic, if you're going to lead me next in a snow removal workout, I'm going to skip the shower until we're all done," I joked as I followed him up the stairs to the kitchen, legs shaky and spent from the workout. "I'll throw on a swipe of deodorant I keep in my purse but that's all the freshness you get."

At the top of the stairs, he turned around and held out his hand as I ascended the last stair. I took it and he drew me in close to him in an embrace. I instinctively put my hands around his neck and he circled my waist with his arms, resting his hands on my lower back. "Syl, sweaty or fresh, I like you all sorts of ways," I suddenly found it difficult to say anything in response as I was feeling turned on by the strength and sweetness rolling off my friend with the realization that I was the object of his affection.

"I loved having you in my bed last night," Nic continued. "I haven't slept that well in a long time, and I was delighted to hear your sweet little breathing noises." Breathing noises? Was that a cutesy way of telling me I was snoring? Whatever. He was right about the rest last night. Before I could answer, both our phones chirped from our pockets. It was from Anna. Our group text to the FSG leadership team read:

FSG will open at noon today to give the City of Fargo a chance to plow streets. See you all at noon.

It was currently 6:45 AM and Nic and I just got the gift of time. We looked at one another, as mischievous smiles spread across our faces. "Well, Mr. Bennett, it seems we have a few more hours to play together."

Nic pulled me in close and this time slid his hands past my low back and cupped my ass in his powerful hands. "Yes and it's always good to spend a little extra time on recovery and bodywork," Nic said in a low husky voice into my ear. "But first we have to refuel," Nic turned away and headed to the kitchen to start making the omelet.

"Hey, you made me dinner last night," I objected. "Let me make breakfast for us," I offered. "OK!" Nic agreed.

***

After our omelets and coffee, I loaded the dishwasher and pressed start. "On second thought, since we don't have to go right into snow work, do you mind if I take that shower now?" I asked

Nic. "No, I don't mind. Do you mind if I join you?" Nic asked hopefully, his blue eyes bright with anticipation. I swallowed, feeling nervous and excited. "Of course you can." We ran up the stairs to the shower and I stripped off my borrowed t-shirt and sweatpants whipping them back behind me playfully at Nic leaving me in only my bra and undies. He peeled off his t-shirt revealing incredible pecs whittled down to his waist, defined abs, and transverse abs creating lines that I could only describe as nature's way of using arrows pointing down to where the action's at down below.

When Nic saw me looking at this area of his body, he slowly removed his athletic shorts and stood in his boxer briefs, thus revealing toned legs and when he turned around I got to enjoy his strong back tapering down as nature's second set of arrows to Nic's strong, muscular, beautiful ass. I squealed in delight at the care Nic took of his body and how I now got to share in the enjoyment of his hard work. Nic moved in closer to me.

"May I help you out of your sweaty bra, Sylvia?" I nodded. Nic reached behind and skillfully released the clasps of my bra and slowly moved the straps off my shoulders and my bra dropped to the floor, revealing my large breasts. Nic let out a little sigh of satisfaction.

He looked in my eyes and I just nodded at him. He leaned in and gave me a long, tender kiss that I felt reignite a fire deep within me that had long been smoldering. He gingerly ran his hands over my breasts, cupped them and placed his head near my right nipple. I lifted my chest higher toward him.

He ran his lips across my nipple, and his warm breath and the sensation of his strong but gentle touch sent goosebumps over my entire body. I placed my hand behind me on the wall to brace myself. He gave my left nipple the same light breath and soft lips treatment before kissing my neck and finding my lips again.

He pressed his body against mine and I bent my knee and placed my foot against the wall behind me to offer some resistance and stability. I felt so wet and turned on as if I was coming alive after being in a sexual sleep state for years.

My hands traced his collarbones and pecs and moved down slowly over each of his rippling abs to the thin line of hair, my very own treasure trail that I traced to the top of his boxer brief line. I paused and looked in his eyes. They were smoldering and yearning, yet at the same time vulnerable and he looked a little scared.

"I'm nervous, Syl. I haven't been intimate with anyone in years," he admitted softly. "Not since I was with my ex-wife." I smiled encouragingly. "In that case we're in this together," I said and he looked surprised. "Andy and I haven't had sex in close to three years," I confessed.

Andy. I felt conflicted feelings rise more strongly within me after hearing myself say his name aloud. I was his wife. We had committed to one another. What was I doing? I didn't want to stop. The feelings were so powerful.

I looked up at Nic. "This is really something I don't want to do, Nic, but I'm going to propose something to you," I said, voice wavering. "Let's not have sex today. Let's have that shower and put one foot in front of another today, and see where our lives take us and how this unfolds." I really wanted to have sex with Nic so badly but I didn't want to self-destruct and I had a family and career to think about, so the stakes were high.

"I agree, Syl," Nic said. "I really like you, and I have for quite some time." Nic pulled my body close to his. I felt his

118

throbbing penis pressing through his boxer briefs and I almost abandoned my proposal and threw him down right there and ravaged him on the floor outside his bathroom.

I reached down and ran my hand down the length of his penis and massaged his testicles and his perineum, as he let out a low satisfied moan in my ear. This was pure ecstasy and I closed my eyes and let this moment burn in my memory.

"I like you too, Dominic Bennett," I said, softly. I took my hands off him and turned into the bathroom and started the shower.

Nic and I spent the next 40 minutes gingerly washing each other's bodies and hair, kissing, and massaging one another. It was so sensual and I didn't feel self-conscious about my body. I felt strong, sexy, and empowered to be taking turns with Nic giving one another gentle kisses.

Nic's body was so incredible but it didn't intimidate me. My mind was so much stronger now, and being able to ask for what I needed and communicate sexually was so refreshing. Nic stepped out of the shower first so he could get me my second set of borrowed clothes. He returned with my fresh clothes and I realized I had sweated through my bra and underwear. Oh well, after the snow moving session, I was headed back home to change into work clothes so I could let my breasts and vagina be free for a few hours.

I joined Nic downstairs and he shared some snow pants and boots with me along with winter gloves and a balaclava. It was a benefit to hang out with someone that had worked in a sporting goods setting for 10 years as there was always plenty of gear on hand. It didn't quite fit but it would do the trick.

"Are you ready to get back to work?" Nic asked as we headed into the garage to get our snow tools. "Yes!" I said.

We worked together as he did the snow blowing and I shoveled the sidewalks. Next we loaded our shovels into the back of his truck and headed back to where my car was stuck in the snowbank at the end of the lane.

We spent the next hour digging out my car and when we freed it, I loaded my purse and clothes from the day before in the back of my car. Nic and I hopped back into his truck for a few minutes while my car warmed up.

"Thank you, Nic, for an incredible night and morning," I said, feeling so much gratitude rise within me that I thought I might cry. "I'll see you at work," I winked at him and flashed him a smile, and hopped out of his truck. "I'll return your snow gear and clothes at work later!"

"Sylvia," Nic said seriously, "I hope this is going somewhere big."

I smiled, blew him a kiss and trudged over to my car, uncertain of what my future held, but happy as hell in the moment.

Chapter 25

"Syl, how did it go with Andy last night?" Roxy cornered me almost immediately when I got to work. "You weren't answering my texts!" She was right about that. I hadn't looked at my phone after making arrangements with Karen and Kenny for the kids and texting Andy that I would talk to him later. The next time was my early morning call from Molly and the alert from Anna that FSG was opening late. Other than that, I was far too busy basking in the pleasure of spending time with Nic to send or receive texts.

"It was...OK," I said. I certainly hadn't had the mental bandwidth to process Andy's request from dinner last night to come home. So much had transpired in the meantime that my head was spinning with the possibility of marriage repair with Andy or the opportunity of starting fresh with Nic.

Either way, it was inappropriate to divulge the nature of Nic and my sexy stormy rendezvous with anyone, including Roxy. Anna would likely make my work life hell if she even suspected something was sparking between Nic and I. It was best to play it safe and cool at work.

"OK?" Roxy pumped for more information.

"Well…" I began, "He wants to come home." Roxy frowned. "What do you think about that?" I paused, considering, and went with my initial gut reaction. "I think not yet."

I was so proud of Andy for the progress he was making but the more I thought about it, the work he had to dig in and do had a lot more to do with himself than it did with me or the kids. I wanted him to be successful and I wanted to hold the line as to what was acceptable in the way he treated me.

"Good choice, Syl." Roxy agreed. I didn't need her to agree with me but it felt good knowing that I was standing firm in my decision that I wasn't going to go right back into a stressful living situation with Andy which would set us up for failure.

I changed the subject. "How was your Valentine's Day, Rox?" Roxy flashed me a huge, mischievous smile. "Lin and I made her favorite Chinese spring rolls and dumplings recipe together, and then watched *Wonder Woman*. After that, we made Amazon warrior fueled love for hours," she finished. "Lin and I still have it going on!"

I smiled and high-fived her. She was right. They really had an incredible connection and you could feel the sparks flying even though they'd been married for five years. They found time to be playful and romantic. At the same time, they both enjoyed their fierce independence and solo activities and hobbies. I have no doubt that this supportive partnership enhanced the quality of their time together. They were the prime example of how to be in a relationship the right way. I aspired to achieve the relationship satisfaction level she and Lin had.

"Good afternoon," Anna appeared in the doorway of Roxy's office. "Sylvia, I'd like to speak with you in my office now," Anna said and quickly strode away down the hall. I hurried after her as Roxy said, "Good luck!" I might need it.

Anna was already seated at her desk when I entered her office. "Have a chair, Sylvia," Anna instructed. "I'll get right to the point," Anna said flatly looking down at a sheet of paper with bullet pointed items.

"There will be some things changing about your job. We're discontinuing in-store men's and women's apparel June thirtieth. We're moving everything online. You'll be overseeing all the orders and shipping and receiving. You'll start to office out of our FSG warehouse location across the river. You'll have the ability to hire a staff of 10 and you'll receive a 10 percent raise," Anna paused to look at me. "I've also approved your vacation for the end of February as you requested. Do you have any questions for me?"

I blinked. I had not expected such a drastic job change but was intrigued by the opportunity for a challenge of getting a new sales platform off the ground and running. This change stirred excitement in me.

"I do have a question, Anna," I said leaning in toward her. "Why me? Why not someone with experience in this area?" Anna pushed back from her desk and leaned back in her chair taking a more casual pose.

"You challenged me, Sylvia," Anna said simply. "You didn't used to challenge me but something has changed within you," she observed. "I told you 'No' on the vacation and you came roaring back in here like I'd kidnapped your baby. You wouldn't back down and you stood up for yourself. It shocked me but I liked it. You're exactly the kind of person I need troubleshooting and building a new service line from scratch."

"Thank you, Anna," I said genuinely. It was the first time since she became my boss that I felt we were on the same page on something and I admired her business acumen. Anna had developed into more of a professional than I'd given her credit for. I reached across the desk and offered my hand for a shake, "I accept. When do I move to my warehouse quarters?"

She smiled. "As soon as you return from your vacation to Colorado. I'll have Human Resources draft your paperwork to reflect your new rate of pay effective March first," she said as she shook my hand to seal the deal. I calculated where I was currently at salary-wise and the 10 percent increase would put me making a little over $85,000 per year. I'd worked hard for FSG and it felt good to be earning at this level.

As I left Anna's office practically floating, I met Nic walking down the hallway toward me. "Good afternoon, Mr. Bennett," I said without slowing my pace. "Ms. Wilde, you look absolutely stunning today," Nic said looking me up and down but not breaking stride either. I was grinning from ear to ear as I headed back to Roxy's office to tell her the good news.

Chapter 26

"I think it's best that we keep up the arrangement we have now," I said as I sat across the table from Andy at a coffee shop. Andy nodded but his shoulders slumped as it wasn't the answer he was hoping for.

It was three days before the kids and I were slated to leave for Colorado. I felt it was important to reach some sort of common ground with my husband. I didn't want him to feel punished for being human and struggling with his addiction. He needed to see his children and vice versa.

"When you guys get back from Colorado, I'd like to spend a week with the kids," Andy said. "I miss them so much, Syl." Tears began to well in Andy's eyes.

"Of course," I said reassuringly. Instinctively, I reached out and put his hand in mine. "I'll ask Roxy if I can stay at her house that week so the kids don't have to go to Cameron's, too."

I paused to think about his time with Cam. "How is that going by the way? Is Eleanor able to put up with you rowdy football buddies from college?"

Andy laughed. "Eleanor hasn't been around. She's on tour. I wouldn't describe our time as rowdy. It's mostly working out, eating well, sleeping well, and going to the library for more self-help books for me these days. Cam said I can stay as long as I want but of course my goal is to get back home sooner rather than later with you and the kids." I nodded but stood firm in my decision to allow more time for him to work on his sobriety.

"Andy, I have exciting news!" I'd almost forgotten to tell him about the job. "FSG is transferring me to the warehouse location and I'll be overseeing the online retail department. I'll cover ordering, shipping and receiving for men's and women's clothing!" I shared excitedly. "It comes with a 10 percent pay raise and I get to hire a staff of 10. Do you think I'll get to drive a forklift?" I asked only half-joking.

"Aww, that's so awesome, Syl," Andy was genuinely excited for me. "When does that start?" I realized the timing of him being with the kids at our house was great as it coincided with my first week on the new job.

Andy and I hugged goodbye and he wished the kids and I well on our trip to Steamboat Springs and asked me to say 'Hi' to my parents from him. My dad and Andy were very close. The strain between Andy and I made my dad feel torn about his love and loyalty to me and his soft spot in his heart for his son-in-law.

"Andy, it's been amazing having Karen and Kenny with me and the kids this winter," I said, deeply appreciative. "I was a little worried at first how all of this would go, but I think it has been so good for Molly and Vinny to get to know them better. They've seemed to come out of their shell with their new responsibilities of grand parenting," I shared. "So despite this being a really hard time, it's awesome to see our friends and family come through in a big way to help us." Andy gathered me up in a big bear hug and whispered in my ear.

"You kicking me out of the house after Christmas likely saved my life, Syl." I buried my head in the familiar embrace of my husband and let myself enjoy this tender moment with him.

Chapter 27

The kids stared out the floor to ceiling windows watching the planes taxiing out and coming in for landings as we waited for seating on our flight to Denver. This was the first time they'd flown on an airplane and they were so excited that even though the plane didn't depart until 10 AM, they were both up at 5 AM, backpacks on and ready to go.

Karen and Kenny were tearful as they helped the kids pack. We'd all grown so much closer to one another over the last two months they'd been staying with us.

"We can stay to make sure the place has eyes on it," Kenny offered. "Oh no, that's fine," I reassured them. "You haven't been home this whole time and you need a break! Plus, you're going to travel part of the month of March. You have some arranging to do at your own home," I reminded them.

I knew staying with us had lit something within my in-laws that had long been dormant. In their own stoic, Norwegian farmer way, they were healing from Carrie's death by allowing themselves to get close to Vinny and Molly.

"Well, we're hopeful Andy continues to improve and that you all can spend time together as a family," Karen added. These were the words that she could use that were as close as she was willing to admit that her son had a drinking problem and unresolved issues of childhood trauma. It would likely take Andy a lot longer to repair his relationship with his parents (and plenty of therapy) than it would to kick the alcohol habit.

"Thank you both so much," I was so grateful for all they had done for us. I wouldn't have been able to maintain my composure at work, and the kids would have had more of a fractured, disrupted day to day routine.

"Andy will be staying here the week we're away and keeping an eye on things."

I knew it would be a test for Andy to be out of Cameron's house and rigid schedule and be able to maintain his sobriety and good habits. I thought it would be a good idea for him to do a trial run while he didn't have the stress of me and the kids as he did a practice adjustment to life back in his home.

I still wasn't convinced that he was ready to come back home and feared moving too quickly would cause him to relapse. I wasn't interested in our children bearing witness to that again.

"Mom, can we go downhill skiing and snowboarding?" Vinny asked as we found our seats on the plane. It would be a three hour flight from Fargo to Denver and then another three hour drive to Steamboat Springs with the kids. I fully expected to be peppered with questions about all the grand mountain adventures we would be participating in the week we were there.

"I think we can start on the bunny hill and see what the ski instructor decides we're capable of doing, buddy," I said tousling his hair. He nodded in agreement with the plan.

I was so excited to be on this trip with the kids and I missed my parents desperately. I was used to my every other day call to them. Having them more than an hour away was hard for me.

"Mommy, can I sit by the window on the way there? Can Vinny can sit by the window on the way back?" Molly asked excitedly. Let the negotiations begin! "Yes," I said quickly so they knew there would be no back and forth about it. I didn't have the strength to mediate arguments between my six and nine-year-old across several states and time zones.

The in-flight movie was a Disney film from a few years ago that I hadn't seen and the kids settled right in to watch. I found myself going into vacation mode and drifting in and out of sleep until I heard the overhead announcement that we'd started our descent into Mile High City.

It was a reminder for me to chug water as to not get dehydrated. I pushed fluids on the kids, too. My little flatlanders and I, whom spent our lives at sea level, had to quickly prepare to acclimate to higher elevation. I didn't need altitude sickness putting a damper on our fun time.

As we descended and my ears popped, I spent some time reflecting on how excited I was to now be living in a body that fully allowed me to enjoy my life. I was closing in on the last 20 to 40 pounds I planned to lose before switching to maintaining my healthy weight for life. If all went well, I'd reach my goal sometime during the summertime, one year after I'd embarked on this journey. I reflected on all that I'd lost and gained through this process of improving my health.

I was so grateful for my body moving me through the years when I carried much more weight. And I was just as grateful for my body's ability to work with me and release the excess that was no longer serving me. I felt like I had a new lease on life and there wasn't anything that was going to stop me.

All of this had come from within me. Nobody rescued me. I rescued myself when I was drowning and spiraling and being self-destructive. I had evidence of my former self that I would carry with me always like tattoos. Loose skin underneath my arms, inner thighs, and lower part of my belly, and stretch marks for being too big for my body.

I didn't care. All of these things were part of my story and reminders of overcoming obstacles and rising up stronger than before. I was able to run long distances and lift heavy weights. I felt that my insides and personality were now a closer match to my outsides.

The icing on the cake was Nic. He'd unlocked a sexual, sensual, playful side of me I thought no longer existed. I was so excited that he would be in Steamboat at the same time as me. I hoped that we'd be able to spend some time together even though he'd be working most of the time at his fitness conference and expo.

I smiled and closed my eyes. I made a mental picture of this moment in time with my children as the wheels touched down on the tarmac. Then, my eyes flashed open to embark on the next leg of my adventure with the kids.

Chapter 28

"Mom! Dad!" I said as I dropped my bags in the front entryway of my parent's condo. I hugged them both hard, acknowledging I was behaving like a small child.

It had been a long day of travel and I was glad to be at my destination. Even though it had only been a few months since Christmas, it felt like an eternity considering all that had happened in my life with Andy.

"Oh my goodness, it is so good to see my babies," my mom gushed, gathering Molly, Vinny, and I all up in a hug.

"How have you been? I told Tom that we shouldn't be away for this long but he likes the mountains so I promised we'd stay when we found out what was going on with Andy," Mom admitted.

She glanced down at the kids, not wanting to say too much about Andy in front of them.

"Anyway, you're here now so who wants some hot chocolate and a snack before we go swim in the pool?" Molly and Vinny shrieked in excitement and followed their grandmother into the kitchen, babbling to her about the mountains they'd driven through on the way here.

My dad cornered me. "Syl, how is Andy?" he asked with concern. I was a little peeved that this was his first question instead of asking how I was doing. However, I respected that they were close, much closer than Andy was with his own father.

"He's getting better, Dad," I said as I took off my jacket and hung it on the hook. I removed and placed my winter boots by the door. I was feeling the exhaustion set in from the day of travel. Additionally, the white-knuckle driving through mountain passes had drained me of energy.

"He's been staying with Cameron and that's been really good for him. He's been completely sober for a little over a month now but had a few slips early on," I admitted. "He's got a lot of work to do on himself, Dad. Some of that I can help him with, but a lot of it is leftover work from processing the death of his sister and repairing his relationship with his own parents."

Dad nodded and looked at the floor. "He's always been such a great guy, Syl. He loves you and the kids so much."

I felt a little twinge of guilt as he said this. I had a tough time believing this considering the dumpster fire of a marriage Andy and I had for the last several years especially.

"Dad, I know you care for Andy." I didn't say more about my feelings for my husband because I was uncertain. I didn't know how capable I was in walking this journey with Andy during his recovery. Only time would tell.

"Who's ready for the pool and hot tub?" Mom, Vinny, and Molly emerged into the living room in their swimsuits, holding their towels.

Both of my kids had hot chocolate moustaches and they appeared to be vibrating with energy. It was apparent my mother had fed them plenty of sugar. These kids would need some pool time to work off all the energy of being cooped up in the plane and in the car. I looked at my watch and it read 7 PM.

"As much as I'd like to run outside, I think I'll wait until the morning to hit the trail as it's pretty dark out," I said. "Do you two mind hanging out with the kids in the pool while I work out at your condo fitness center?"

Mom beamed at me. "First of all, Sylvia, you look absolutely amazing!" I smiled and did a little twirl.

"My mom honors her body every day by moving well and fueling well," Molly chimed in with her cute little voice. It was something I said often to the children about moving and fueling well to have the best quality of life. It was fun to hear that parroted back at me. It felt good to have a positive influence on my children's inner dialogue.

My parents took the kids to the pool, and I went to the fitness center on the top floor of the building with floor-to-ceiling windows that overlooked the mountains. I could see the twinkling lights and spotlight of a ski resort in the distance. I could make out the little ants of people that were riding the lifts up and skiing down.

I couldn't wait to take my children to the ski hill so we could all try this new sporting adventure together. I led myself in a nice, sweaty, hour-long dumbbell/cardio workout. I added an extra-long stretch session at the end to shake out the stiffness of a day in cramped spaces. I chugged a ton of water and as I was preparing to leave, I felt the buzz of my phone in my pocket. I felt myself warm with excitement. It read:

Nic: How's it going, Mountain Mama? Are you in Steamboat? I hope the trip went well.

I smiled and tapped out a response:

Sylvia: It's great! The kids are swimming with my folks, and I got in a sweaty workout. How's the conference?

Nic: Wonderful but I'm having a hard time concentrating knowing that you're in the same place as me. When can I see you?

Sylvia: I want to spend a few days catching up with my folks but they know I have a friend in town from work, so how about Friday? Maybe into Saturday? :)

Nic: Friend in town, eh?;) Yes, my conference ends on Friday at noon but I don't fly back to Fargo until Sunday. I have an idea. Are your parents able to watch the kids overnight?

Sylvia: Yes.

Nic: Then one-night mountain adventure it is. Can you meet me at my hotel conference center at 3 PM Friday? Bring your outdoor gear and a swimsuit. I'll bring food and bedding.

Sylvia: I'm very intrigued! Where are we going?

Nic: It's a surprise. :) Have a great few days with your family and I'll see you Friday!

I could barely wait. Where was he going to take me? It had been so long since I'd been on an adventure. I was all of a sudden very glad Roxy and I went on a quick trip to Minneapolis last weekend. It was a lovely trip with her and I scored two awesome new swimsuits. I found it hard to keep the secret of seeing Nic while in Steamboat from my best friend.

Roxy was a very perceptive and intuitive person. If she so much as caught a whiff of a suspicious situation, she was all over that, interrogating her suspects until she got answers. I kept our conversation light and focused on her and ultramarathon training.

She was planning on the Grand Canyon Ultra coming up in May and though she'd completed the 50 mile distance, which had been in Minnesota, she hadn't done this race at higher elevation. I hadn't told her yet, but I planned to surprise her and Lin by traveling to Arizona to support her on race day.

I let myself back into the condo and donned one of my two new swimsuits. It was a lovely gunmetal grey number with a halter top and two-tone greys. Simple yet stunning and my height and work in the gym made me feel like a statuesque Amazon warrior in it.

My parents and kids were still swimming, so I ran from the side and did a cannonball into the pool. The kids giggled with excitement. I'm not sure they'd ever known me to be this active and playful with them. They were loving every minute of it.

Chapter 29

"Mom, I'm doing it!" Vinny shouted proudly to me from the bunny hill at the Steamboat Resort.

It was only 11 AM and he was rocking the ski lessons. He was a very naturally athletic kid and had taken the coaching to heart. He was almost ready to level up and ride the chair lift to ski the next challenging hill.

Molly, on the other hand, went with my dad and spent the last two hours going down the snow tube hill over and over again. He was such a good sport. My mom and I walked around the grounds bouncing between Molly and Vinny and catching up with each other.

"Sylvia, what are you going to do?" Mom asked bluntly. "Are you going to leave him when he's trying so hard to get better?"

She was obviously making her feelings known about what she thought I should do with my life. I was a little annoyed but understood that she only knew long-term monogamy. Despite their run of the mill fight, my mom and dad had always been on a fairly even keel with one another. Neither of them struggled with addiction other than showing their love with food. However, that was a fairly normal affliction with Midwesterners.

"I don't know, Mom," I said honestly.

It was true that Andy was working very hard. I didn't know how to navigate this and my time spent with Nic was complicating things further.

"Do you love him, Sylvia?" This question from her made my heart skip a beat. I spent a few moments thinking before I answered.

"I don't know, Mom."

It hurt to admit I wasn't sure about my feelings for my husband. We'd been disconnected from one another for so long. Now that our marriage was being tested, I felt both Andy and I would be capable of making our way through this world on our own. We'd proven this over the last few months spent apart from one another.

The prospect of being on my own scared me because it would mean turning the kids' lives upside down. Their current understanding of the situation was that Dad was spending a lot of time working on his health to kick his alcohol addiction.

I was very honest with them about the disease of alcoholism. I shared that it would take their dad time to get healthy again. They were very understanding as they likened it to my journey through weight loss and healthier eating habits. They observed it had taken me close to nine months to make progress. I also let them know that once any goal in anyone's life is achieved, it then takes a lifetime of work to maintain and improve upon that goal.

I knew I was a strong, capable woman able to take care of myself and my kids. It just felt like somewhat of a failure to have a marriage end. Especially after spending so many years with Andy.

We'd been Andy and Sylvia since high school. We'd both be responsible for redeveloping our individual identities outside of one another. Initially there was a strong sense in me to rescue Andy from the circumstances of his life. Now, I didn't have the emotional bandwidth to do that heavy work any longer.

I felt so badly that he had lost his one and only sibling so tragically. I wanted to help him fill up all those sad, empty, broken, angry spaces with my love. However, by doing that, I had inadvertently allowed him to not fully dig in and do the work of healing. And in doing so, I lost myself along the way, and my own sense of identity.

"Mommy, I'm hungry!" I was pulled back to reality by Molly tugging on my hand leading me toward the chalet. "I want hot cocoa, and a giant hot pretzel with cheese sauce dip."

My mom, dad, and I shook our heads and giggled. "And a side of apple slices and baby carrots," I added holding the line. The kids knew that snacks were allowed but balance was key to their energy and performance. It was an uphill battle with all the junk food they were offered in school, at birthday parties, and from grandparents, but I would repeat myself until I was blue in the face so my children knew and understood how food fueled their bodies.

"You three go ahead and order," I said breaking away to head back to the ski hill to watch Vinny do a run before making him take a lunch break. Vinny was skiing like a pro already and even got me with snow spray when he came to a stop in front of me, a huge grin spreading across his face.

He looked so much like Andy. Big brown eyes, dimples, tall, and muscular already.

"Are you ready to get some grub, champ?" I asked.

"Yes, I'd like a cheeseburger, fries, and a Coke," he responded. OK, so clearly more work to be done in the nutrition department with the children.

"Let's do a cheeseburger, carrots, apples, and chocolate milk," I countered.

"Deal!" Vinny said, unbinding his ski boots from the skis, and clomping ahead of me into the chalet to join the grandparents.

As I was finishing my chicken taco salad, I felt the buzz of a text message in my pocket. I pulled out my phone and read my new text.

Cameron: Have you heard from Andy?

Sylvia: No, I haven't. Why?

Cameron: I just got a weird text message from him. It said that he found men's clothing at your house and he wants to start drinking again.

"Damn it!" I thought to myself. I'd washed and dried Nic's clothes from the snowstorm night I spent at his house and placed the clothes in my gym bag so I'd remember to return them. Andy must have found them when staying at the house. I was not prepared to discuss Nic with Andy and this may have moved up the timeline of me having that conversation with my husband.

Sylvia: I'll give Andy a call and check in with him. Thanks for all you do, Cam.

Cameron: No problem, Syl. Anything for you and Andy and the kids. Take care of you.

"Hey guys, I'm going to call your dad and check in and see how everything is going in Fargo, OK?"

My mom and dad gave me a suspicious look but the kids were blissfully unaware as they devoured their food and told stories about their morning on the slopes.

"Tell Daddy I love him," said Molly.

"Yeah, and tell Dad I'm an expert skier," added Vinny.

Stepping out of the chalet and into the sunlight, I dialed Andy. When he picked up, I could hear the thickness in his voice. He'd been drinking.

"So you've moved on, Sylvia," Andy said coldly. "That didn't take you long."

"Andy, don't do this," I said. "You don't have to throw away all your hard work," I encouraged. He laughed at the other end of the line.

"All my work was to prove to you that I was loyal to the family and meanwhile, the second I'm out of the house you're fucking anyone with a pulse."

Well, it didn't take long for mean, drunk Andy to return. My eyes darted around as I looked for a more private area to talk. I walked the length of the wrap-around deck of the chalet. I found a place to sit watching the skiers finish their runs. Then, they'd hop back on the lift and ride up the mountain to go again.

"Will you give me a chance to explain?" I remained calm because I wasn't going to let Andy's emotional instability derail what I needed to say.

"It doesn't matter, Sylvia. Our marriage was dead years ago." Andy said. "You don't have to pretend to love me for the sake of the children," Andy sounded so sad and defeated.

"Andy, I don't know what to say," I was fumbling over what I could or should say. I didn't feel like I should comfort him, plus I didn't even know if he'd remember this conversation depending on how intoxicated he was.

"Let me help you in that case, Syl," Andy said. "I want a divorce. We're done. We'll start the paperwork when you get back." I heard a click on the other end of the line. I kept the phone up to my ear even though Andy was gone.

Chapter 30

I returned to my parents and kids at their lunch table and I could tell my mother knew something was wrong. I'd opted to shove the conversation to the back of my mind for the afternoon.

After lunch, Molly, Vinny and I tried our hand at snowboarding. It truly was a ton of fun and I am proud of the kids for trying so many new things. I was also impressed with my body, especially my leg and core strength for keeping me up on the board. I wasn't ready to do the Olympic trials yet, but I did remain uninjured and enjoyed myself so that was a win.

That evening, we wound down playing in the pool and relaxing in the hot tub back at my parent's condo and the kids tipped over at 8 PM, exhausted from their day of adventure.

"Spill the beans," My mother cornered me after I'd tucked in the kids and kissed them goodnight. "What did Andy say to you? You looked like you'd seen a ghost when you came back in the chalet today."

I sighed and tears sprang to my eyes. I reached out to my mother for a hug and buried my head in her neck and started to cry.

She patted my back and stroked my hair just like when I was a little girl.

"There, there, Syl," she cooed soothingly. "It's all going to be alright."

"Mom, he asked me for a divorce," I said through sobs. "I could tell he had been drinking and he found men's clothes at the house and he lost it." My mother pushed me away at arm's length.

"What were men's clothes doing at your house?" My shoulders dropped and I told her the story from Valentine's Day and getting my car stuck and my night with Nic. Mom got really quiet.

"Are you going to say anything?" I pleaded.

"Sylvia, you've been under so much pressure and have been carrying a heavy load of motherhood, your career, and have kept up your strength to persevere through it all," she observed.

"It's natural that you would enjoy a man's affections, especially after the tough years of marriage you've had and the lack of love shown to you by your husband," she paused.

"It's just that the timing of all of this isn't great. Andy feels deeply betrayed by you. He's trying to get better and this has obviously derailed him."

I looked up at her. "Mom, there's something else," I said voice shaking.

"It was a relief to hear those words from Andy," I admitted. "I felt like a weight had been lifted. Even though this is painful, it feels like I don't have to carry the success of this dysfunctional marriage any longer. I think in the long run that this divorce will be good for all four of us in our family."

My mom nodded, sadly. "Sylvia, you're so much braver and courageous than I ever have been," she said, tears welling in her eyes.

"You only get this one beautiful, messy life and I support you in cultivating the best version of your life possible." I hugged her and gave her permission to share with my dad who had already gone to bed. Molly had tired him out on the snow tube hill earlier in the day.

"Mom, thank you for being my cheerleader."

"Sylvia, one more question," she said as she turned back from walking down the hall away from me. "Is your friend in town that you're meeting with Friday into Saturday, Nic?" she asked pointedly. She'd connected the dots of my excitement surrounding my adventure tomorrow. I nodded. She gave me a small smile.

"Guard your heart, child," she said. "Don't give away too much of your strength, beauty, and precious self. Any man that has the luxury of spending time with you should realize it's a privilege to do so." I walked back to her and gave her a long, gratitude-filled hug before falling into bed, exhausted.

***

I left at sunrise the next morning to explore Steamboat on foot. I needed to clear my mind from the disruptive phone call with Andy the day before. As I ran through the quiet streets of the sleepy ski town, I reflected on how much I was willing to share with Nic tonight.

I didn't want to share everything about the turmoil going on in my personal life. I also had no interest in Nic feeling like he had to play any significant role in my life. There was no need for him to step up and be my boyfriend or caregiver.

I just wanted to have fun, make memories in the mountains, and keep it light and simple. I would need a lot of solo time as I rediscovered my identity outside of being in a marriage.

I would also have to focus on the well-being of the kids. My hope is they could come out of this life-changing event of not having their dad around all the time as unscathed as possible. I had a sick feeling wondering if Andy would fight me for custody of the kids.

I quickly pushed that thought aside. There was nothing I could do about how he reacted to the situation. Even if it meant lawyers, debt, humiliation, and hard times. I was willing to go down the rabbit hole to be free and healthy on the other side of this.

Chapter 31

The kids and I went back to the ski resort on Friday morning. Molly wanted to go tubing again, but with my mom this time, and Vinny went skiing and snowboarding. I decided to try out skiing, too. I wasn't bad at all. I was worried that after snowboarding the day before, I would be too sore to ski. However, I was hanging in there on the ski runs with Vinny even after a sunrise six mile run that morning.

Vinny and I had a grand time riding the chair lift and catching up with each other. He was definitely a better skier than me already. I made a mental note to take him to Minneapolis before the snow melted completely. He would enjoy another ski and snowboard adventure. I thought it might be a good guy's getaway for Andy and Vinny.

Thinking about Andy made me sad. I was disappointed that he'd turned so quickly to alcohol when faced with problems. I also wondered how his body was tolerating alcohol after being sober for the better part of two months. I took a deep breath and realized that those were worries I didn't need to carry with me any longer.

I admit I was worried about his behavior swings. If his drinking kept up, I'd have to work with the lawyers to make sure our kids were safe when they were in his care. I tried to push these scary future scenarios out of my mind. It was all hypothetical and truly out of my control.

We all rendezvoused back at the chalet at noon for lunch together. We were all ravenously hungry and scarfed down our food. As the kids finished up, I pulled out my phone to send Andy a text.

Sylvia: Andy, I know this is a difficult time, but we will get through it.

Please be safe with yourself.

A few minutes later, I received a text back from him.

Andy: Whatever, Sylvia, you broke my heart. Tell the kids I love them.

I felt my body go cold. He was so angry with me. I sighed and realized this would be a hard road navigating divorce with him. I wasn't going to let this future turmoil ruin the rest of my vacation. I began to put my phone away and then realized I needed to make a plan with Nic for tonight.

Sylvia: Just to confirm, I'm still meeting you at 3 PM with my swimsuit and snow gear for our overnight, correct?

Nic texted back almost immediately.

Nic: That's right! Can you get a ride to the Steamboat Grand? I have a Toyota 4Runner with the rest of our gear packed and ready to go.

Sylvia: Yes, I'll meet you in the lobby at 3.

I put my phone away and finished lunch with the kids, basking in their excitement. Seeing the look of enjoyment on my mom and dad's faces as they spent time with their grandkids was gratifying, too. I was so fortunate to have all four of the kids' grandparents involved in their lives.

***

I hugged and kissed the kids and left them with my dad while my mom drove me to Nic's hotel. "I can barely endorse this, Sylvia," my mother said. "However, you deserve to have some fun, and I can't stop you from making this choice. You're a grown woman." I smiled at her.

"Mom, I really appreciate you and dad taking the kids overnight. And thank you for not making me feel bad about taking some time for me."

I hugged her and stepped out of the car to retrieve my backpack loaded with my gear. I came to the driver's side door and tapped on her window. She rolled her window down.

"I just want you to know that I haven't felt this alive in years," I said as if to justify this time for myself and Nic to her.

She smiled at me. "You look fabulous in your new swimsuits, Syl. Use condoms, my dear, and don't be stupid."

My mouth dropped open as she drove away. That was more sex education she'd shared with me in the entirety of my years living with her. Her layers were being peeled back now that she was in her sixties. She was getting feisty and I liked it.

I walked in through the sliding doors of the Steamboat Grand and spotted Nic. He stood from where he was seated in the rustic-looking chair next to the fireplace. He smiled broadly at me and his blue eyes were even brighter than I remembered.

Butterflies flooded my stomach and we each walked halfway toward one another. We met in an embrace and I felt my uncertainty and burden about my future melt away in his strong arms. I made a vow not to discuss my personal life for the entirety of our time together.

He held me back from him. "Sylvia, where we're going, there isn't going to be cell service. You might want to let your parents and your kids know so they don't worry. I let Sarah and my kids know as well."

"Do you plan to kill me?" I asked in a deadpan voice. He looked confused. "I'm kidding, Nic." He smiled and shook his head at me.

"Let me send a few texts and then shut my phone down so it doesn't roam and drain the battery." I texted my mom that I would be going off the grid.

I texted Andy and let him know that if wanted to get in touch with the kids, he could reach them through my parents. Moments later, I got a text back from my Mom acknowledging that she wouldn't be able to reach me. She let me know Andy could get ahold of her if he wanted to chat with the kids.

I received a garbled text from Andy with misspellings and expletives. So he was for sure back on the bottle. Well, I tried to communicate. It was up to him what he did with that. I turned my phone off.

"Ready to ascend that mountain with me?" Nic asked pointing to a tall peak off in the distance.

"Ready!" I said.

Nic reached for my hand and we headed outside to the vehicle.

Chapter 32

Nic and I made our way up the mountain and arrived at our destination 20 minutes later. The sign at the entrance read, "Strawberry Park Hot Springs." I squealed with delight. I had read about this place in the guidebook but knew that the kids would likely get too hot in the springs and lose interest quickly. I had put it out of my mind for this trip.

Nic had scored major points in my book by bringing me here. I appreciated that he knew me well enough to know that I preferred to be off the grid eating out of a cooler, hiking around and exploring, and soaking in the natural springs.

"What do you think, Sylvia?" he said as we arrived on foot hauling our gear through the snow. I was standing in front of a train caboose converted into a tiny cabin. It was phenomenal.

"This is amazing, Nic!"

I was so thrilled to be on this adventure with him. We loaded in our cooler, sleeping gear, overnight bags, and got settled in. We took a moment to rest on the futon together.

"I realize this isn't a four-star hotel, Syl," Nic said.

"You're right. It's better," I said as I leaned in to kiss him.

I placed my hand on his chest and ran my fingers down his breastbone and back and forth across his amazingly strong pecs and encircling each of his nipples with my index finger.

"Can you take this off, please?" I said gently tugging on his long sleeve t-shirt. He obliged by sitting up, removing his shirt, and returning to his spot next to me.

I nudged his shoulder to make him lie flat on his back and got myself up on all fours above him. I began by slowly kissing his right ear and moving down his neck and placing kisses along his right collarbone. I continued to graze my lips past the bulge of his pectoral muscle drawing his nipple into my mouth and encircling it with my tongue.

He let out a small satisfied moan and reached his hands up to cup my ample breasts through my shirt. I moved back up and gave him a deep, passionate kiss. I decided to see if he liked a little lick followed by a nibble on his left ear. Based on the noises he was making, the answer was 'Yes.'

I rose up off my hands and removed my sweatshirt and bra. I let my large breasts spill out and Nic said, "You're so beautiful, Sylvia." I flashed him a smile and placed my breasts atop his pecs and slowly moved myself along the length of his upper torso, letting my breasts feel the indentations of his abdominal muscles all the way down to the top of his jeans. I was so turned on, but I wanted to make all of this last and burn it into my memory.

I rubbed my breasts along the ridge in his jeans and paused to look up at him and pointed to the prominent bulge where I had rested my breasts.

"May I get in here?" Nic nodded and lightly thrashed his legs around in delighted anticipation. I slowly unbuttoned and unzipped his jeans and tugged them down to his knees exposing his blue boxer briefs. I slowly lifted the last article of clothing that separated me from Nic's beautiful cock and pulled his boxer briefs down to his knees to join the jeans.

I spent a moment using my finger pads to slowly stroke Nic's thick, veiny cock as it throbbed beneath my touch.

I kissed along the lines of the front side of Nic's hips making my way down, past his cock to kiss his groin and inner thighs on both sides.

I needed him to know I was going to take my time and be respectful and careful with him. I wanted to savor his beautiful physique.

"Should we see if they like each other?" I asked playfully as I pointed to my breasts and his penis. "I think that's a great idea, Syl," Nic said with a sly smile.

I brought my fingers to my mouth and soaked them with my tongue. I wet my breastbone running my fingers slowly between my breasts. I then leaned over Nic's cock. I encased him in my pendulous breasts with a tight, wet fit.

I bounced up and down on his cock with my breasts until Nic said, "Oh Syl, I might not be able to hold back much longer. I want to give you pleasure, too."

I backed off his cock as requested and said, "Oh, you'll get your chance."

I moved to position myself from the side of him to right in between his legs. I paused and looked up at him.

"Nic, we can't come back from here," I said honestly. "This changes things."

He nodded and stroked my hair. "I know, Syl, we'll take it slowly, OK? Either one of us can slow it down or speed it up," he said. "Our lives aren't simple, but I love the way I feel when I'm with you."

"OK, one more thing," He raised his eyebrows. "Are you healthy sexually? Do you have any STDs? I've only had sex with one person and I don't have anything," I shared.

"Me too," Nic said with a smile. "I met Sarah in college and she was my only sexual partner. I have a clean bill of health, Syl. Thanks for sharing and making sure I'm healthy, too. I really respect that. Oh, and I had a vasectomy a year after Sammy was born, too. No more kids for me." Nic pulled me toward him and kissed me deeply in appreciation.

I moved back down toward the middle of his beautiful body and opened my mouth and drew his penis in slowly, savoring the way the softness of his skin juxtaposed with the throbbing vascularity of his cock.

He let out a moan and squirmed beneath me in deep pleasure. I could feel my own self get heated up between my legs, but I planned to be patient with my needs. I had waited a very long time to have exceptional sex. I didn't want to rush through the process.

I worked on his cock like it was my full-time job. I challenged myself to see if I could open my mouth wider and angle my jaw in a way that I could take in his penis all the way back deep into my throat and touch my lips to the base where his cock met his mons pubis.

I could, and Nic was clearly enjoying my skills. I took Nic's penis out of my mouth to make sure to give his testicles a little love, too. I placed one and then both of them in my mouth and used my tongue in a circular motion on him while stroking his cock.

I took his cock back into my mouth. I then used both hands to lightly jack him off while sucking on him so I could watch his face. I could feel he was getting close to the edge. He opened his eyes and put his hand on my cheek as he ejaculated his sweet and salty self down my throat. I swallowed, satisfied, and made my way back up to cuddle next to him.

"Oh, Sylvia." Nic said, breathing heavily, a glisten of sweat on his forehead. "That was amazing. Thank you for being so generous with yourself, sweetheart." I filled with warmth and snuggled in closer to him, one of my breasts pushed into the side of him and the other resting on his chest.

"Do you mind if I return the favor?" Nic asked eagerly.

"Actually, I do," I said. "I am hungry and I want to go exploring!"

Nic laughed. "In that case, I'll make you some dinner for all that hard work you did," Nic said winking at me. "I need to build up my energy again, too, if I'm going to keep up with you."

Nic and I both dressed and he turned on some music from a small CD player he brought on the trip. He started by playing a mix CD of 80s tunes. It was delightful. He shooed me out of our caboose cabin home for the night to go look around the park while he made dinner.

The sun was setting as I headed outside. I looked all around me and took in the sights of snow-covered peaks in the distance and the mist rising up from the hot springs. It was an idyllic sight. I felt as if I were in a postcard.

A twinge of guilt crept in as I hiked to the bathroom facilities. I tried to shake the shame I felt betraying Andy by being with Nic right now. I took a deep breath and let those feelings go. I wasn't going to let the burden of tomorrow's worries rob me of the joy, happiness, and pleasure I was feeling now.

I freshened up my deodorant, brushed my hair, and changed into my swimsuit. I figured we'd enjoy the hot springs after dinner and I wanted to be ready. I glanced in the mirror and smiled at myself, filled with self-love. I was make-up free and thought I hadn't looked this beautiful and fresh in years.

I could see my jawline and collar bones were beginning to emerge as my layers of fat had slowly gone away. My hard work and dedication to my body and mind over the last nine months was apparent.

I would have never predicted where I was today, if you asked me last spring. Before, I was merely an observer in my own life. I had been moving through my life aimlessly, instead of being in the driver's seat.

I had a new job challenge on the horizon. I had to dig in and do the hard work of guiding myself and the children through the end of my marriage to Andy. I felt, at this moment at least, ready for the battle ahead. With my daily discipline of commitment to myself, and the help from friends and family, I would make it through this

unexpected season of my life.

Chapter 33

Nic prepared peanut butter and jelly sandwiches for dinner for us. He used thick, homemade bread he'd purchased at the bakery in Steamboat. He added sliced apples and baby carrots on the side. We were so hungry. We devoured our meal quickly and made all the happy feeding noises. We both chugged our bottles of water, not wanting altitude sickness to hamper our good time.

He and I were both very excited eaters. We agreed and laughed about how our approach to food was similar to both adventure and sex. In one word: enthusiastic.

Nic and I put on stocking caps, sweatshirts and sweatpants over our swimsuits, and added wool socks and boots. We grabbed our towels and headed out of the caboose to soak in the hot springs. We each had a headlamp as it was pitch dark now at 7 PM. It was so still, quiet, and serene.

"Sylvia, do you want to stay near the top of the springs, or hike down to the lower springs?" Nic asked.

I noticed there were more guests milling about and soaking at the upper springs. I suggested we go down to the lower springs. We hiked down and found a natural pool that was empty.

We stripped down to our swimsuits and clicked off our headlamps. The only sounds were the whirring of the natural springs flowing. I held onto the railing and descended step by delicious step into the warm water and let it envelop me.

The springs came up to my waist but I squatted down in the hot water to keep myself warm all the way up to my neck. I felt Nic come up behind me and kneel and pick me up underwater and then he sat back down on the stone bench and placed me on his lap.

I put my arms around his neck and we both looked up at the incredible display of stars overhead. After a few moments, we saw a shooting star light up the sky and then go dark. "I planned that," Nic said. "Right," I said, laughing. "You really know how to sweep a girl off her feet." Nic leaned in and kissed me.

I hopped off his lap and swam to the opposite end of the warm pool. "Where'd you go?" Nic said after a minute. I swam back toward him and hopped back on his lap. "Oh my," Nic said, feeling my body. I had shimmied out of my swimsuit and left it at the opposite end of the pool.

Feeling the warm water on my body underneath the mountain sky made me feel so light and free, content, and fulfilled. Nic's hands explored my body underwater and he tilted me back in his left arm while he used his right hand to caress my inner thighs. I held my breath as Nic paused his hand in between my legs to stroke my outer labia and move more inward near the top and gently, lightly massage my clitoris.

"Breathe, darling," Nic whispered in my ear. I let out my breath I'd been holding.

I pressed my hips toward his hands as he continued to work on satisfying me. He angled his hand so he could slip two fingers to gently pump in and out of my vagina rhythmically. He used his thumb to put just the right amount of pressure on my clitoris.

I placed my heels on the ledge on the other side of Nic to thrust my body harder into Nic's hand and felt myself building until I couldn't hold it in anymore. I covered my mouth and tried to muffle my satisfied, whimpering noises. I wished to not draw attention from the higher hot spring's guests to our sexcapade. I nuzzled into Nic's neck as I came hard into his hand.

Nic gently drew his fingers out of me and moved his hand along my belly and breasts. I arched my back so my nipples pressed out of the water. The water glistened on them from the reflection of the moon.

"Wow," Nic said. "You're so beautiful and sexy. I'm in the company of a goddess." I rolled off his lap into the water and stood up striking a warrior pose. He laughed and shook his head. "And you're playful and funny."

"That was incredible, Nic," I said. "Thank you for being so adventurous. This was exciting, dangerous, and voyeuristic," I admitted.

"Speaking of, I'm going to get my swimsuit before we get kicked off the property," I said and swam back to where I'd abandoned my garment on the other side of the hot spring enclosure.

Nic and I spent a little more time splashing around and stargazing and talking about everything and nothing. I snapped a mental picture of this incredible moment in time.

Our time together was so tender and sweet, I wanted to treat it with kid gloves. I knew my life was about to become very complicated. I didn't want to ruin the sanctity of this moment with thoughts of what I had to return to in Fargo.

When we got out of the springs, we toweled off, dressed, and hiked back to our caboose cabin. We grabbed our toiletries and walked to the restroom/shower facilities to get ready for bed.

As we settled in for the night, we ate some beef jerky, nuts and raisins and danced around to some 80s tunes from Nic's CD collection. We then snuggled into our futon sleeping bag arrangement and told stories. We shared about our childhood experiences, our siblings and families, and told a few funny work stories.

We'd had our share of wild customer requests we'd received over the years. We drifted off in each other's arms and I wasn't sure if I'd ever had such a romantic, perfect time. I could only hope that Nic and I got the opportunity to have many more times together like this.

Chapter 34

"Good morning, sunshine!" Nic said as I stretched and rolled over in the sleeping bag. "Hey there, handsome!" I smiled and stretched and got out of bed feeling incredibly rested and serene.

Nic was making eggs and bacon on the hot plate, with toast and jam on the side.

"Want to fuel up for a morning hike?" Nic asked.

"You bet I do! I'm going to run up to the bathroom quickly to change into my gear, put in my contacts, and brush my teeth because Wonder Woman doesn't wake up ready to go; it's a process," I joked.

He smiled. "I appreciate your honesty. It's refreshing to know that Wonder Woman needs some prep time to be awesome," Nic said with a wink.

I stepped outside and was immediately rewarded with an incredible sunrise. There wasn't a cloud in the sky. The steam mist was rising off the natural hot springs into the air with the snow-capped mountains in the background. I closed my eyes and lifted my face skyward to soak in everything about this spectacular adventure.

Upon my return to the caboose, I was met by a shirtless Nic offering me breakfast. I stood in the doorway smiling, checking him out. He noticed my wandering eyes traversing the full expanse of his body and gave me a slow twirl.

"Cute butt," I said and took my plate from him. "Do I have to take my shirt off, too, to eat breakfast?"

He laughed. "Shirts are completely optional here at the caboose bed and breakfast." I shrugged, set down my plate and took off my shirt and bra and then went right back to eating.

Nic shook his head in amazement at my comfortability around him.

"Sylvia, you are so much fun. I love that you're uninhibited and playful. You bring out the best in me."

I cocked my head to the side and asked, "Is there a worst in you, Nic?"

He was thoughtful before he answered. "No, not necessarily. I forget to have fun. I go to work, work out, and eat the same food day after day. Then, I pour myself into enjoying my kids when I'm with them, and forget to be silly and lighten up," he admitted. "Thank you for showing me how to enjoy the moment."

I raised my glass of orange juice to toast our success. "To lightening up together, Nic!"

I added, "And I win lightening up because I took 80 pounds off my frame this past year. This has certainly contributed to my positive mood," I admitted.

"Cheers to that!" Nic said excitedly. "You look fabulous, Sylvia. I've always thought you've looked great even when you were a bigger version of yourself. Now your confidence, kindness, and sexiness flow freely. I'm a huge fan."

After breakfast, Nic and I headed back to the main road into Strawberry Park to hike. We descended for an hour winding down the road. It took us an hour and a half to ascend back to where we started.

We were simultaneously chilled and sweaty underneath our winter gear from the work our bodies did carrying us up and down the mountain. When we returned to the caboose cabin, we agreed that it was a good time to have a final soak in the springs together.

"Nic, do I have to wear my swimsuit this time?" I joked, considering it was broad daylight.

"You do you, lady!" Nic said.

We soaked, floated, stretched, and drank our water in the hot spring in silence. Nic was the first to speak.

"Can I ask you something, Sylvia, and can you please be honest with me?" I looked in his eyes and saw that they looked a little vulnerable and scared. This surprised me considering he was such a strong man.

"Of course, Nic." I said moving nearer to him so he knew he had my full attention.

"What can I expect next?" He asked. "I mean, how do we want to play this when we return to Fargo?" He gestured with his pointer finger to indicate us as a romantic item. I looked away and watched the steam rise off the springs.

"I honestly don't know exactly what this will look like, Nic," I admitted. I figured since Nic had asked, I might as well share the last thing Andy said to me on the phone a few days ago.

"Andy asked me for a divorce," I shared, averting my eyes from Nic's gaze. "Although that is a good thing for us, it will be a tough road for the kids and I as we navigate this," I said as I looked up to lock eyes with Nic. His expression was one of genuine care and concern.

"My children are my first priority, Nic, so I want to be there and help them process this big change," I continued. "I fear I'll be tossed into chaos and uncertainty when I return to Fargo." I sighed. "I just can't say what my life will look like even a month from now."

Nic nodded and pulled me onto his lap and held me close. "I'll wait, Sylvia," he said softly. "I'll show up when you need me, and I'll give you space when you don't. I want you to know that I respect your independence. I understand you need to go through this stormy time, but you do not have to go through this by yourself. Even though we've recently become romantic, I am your friend first and always."

I was speechless. I'd never been treated like this by a man before. I'd always felt I needed to justify and prove myself to men. It had been the case that I had to give something to get something in my relationship with Andy. It was all a big game of scorekeeping and transactions.

I was so thankful for the ease of communication that flowed freely between Nic and I. It was truly a gift.

I hugged him, and whispered in his ear, "Dominic Bennett, I am so grateful you are in my life. Thank you for being you."

I shifted back to look him in the eyes, "Now take me to bed or lose me forever," I said, quoting the Meg Ryan line from *Top Gun*. Nic smiled broadly. The spark and fire returning to his big blue eyes, he responded with his line as Goose, "Show me the way home, honey."

Chapter 35

Nic and I were so hungry for one another when we got back into the caboose cabin, we stripped off our clothes and swimsuits and left them in a pile by the door. Our earlier escapades were marked by patience and a slow cadence and build; this one was more frenzied and aggressive. There was a stronger urgency and need.

I laid back on the futon and spread my legs wide, my vagina fully on display for Nic to see. He bent down and began exploring me with his tongue and I had to reach back and hold on to the wooden frame of the futon to contain myself from the incredible sensations of him going down on me. I really wanted his cock inside me to fill me and I wanted to hold on to my orgasm. I let him lick me for a few minutes and then gently tapped his head. He looked up at me.

"Nic, I need you inside me," I said breathlessly.

"Gladly," he responded, moving to hover over me. I felt just the tip of his penis at the base of my vagina barely entering me as I was swollen and engorged with wanting. I moaned in anticipation as Nic slowly entered more and more of his girthy cock into me until he was thrusting deeply and rhythmically all the way in. I was experiencing so much ecstasy, I felt like I was floating above my body as my orgasm built.

"Oh Nic, I can't hold out any longer," I said breathlessly.

"Please don't," Nic said. "I want to feel you come on me." That's all I needed to hear. I exploded, and thrashed, and pressed my body hard against his cock as my orgasm tore through my body. Nic reached climax shortly after and I satisfyingly felt the aftershocks of his orgasm. We slowly rocked ourselves together back to baseline.

As we laid in silence cuddling afterward, I whispered, "Those are my favorite chemicals. The ones I feel during orgasm. Like a fireworks show in my brain."

Nic agreed. "Sylvia, thank you so much for helping me find my sexual self again."

I smiled. "You're so welcome, Mr. Bennett. The feeling is 100 percent mutual. My sexual self is wide awake. I don't want her to go back to sleep any time soon."

Nic and I slowly began getting ready as our adventure in the mountains was drawing to a close. I packed my backpack and took one last trip up to the showers to ready myself for my return to life as a mom and career professional.

I would also soon hold a new title; divorcee. I didn't want to think about what that would entail. With the help of my parents and Roxy, all would turn out OK. I let myself mourn the loss of my marriage as I cried in the shower.

I hoped that Andy would find the strength to beat his addiction and overcome the trauma of his childhood. Even though our relationship fizzled, I only wished the best for him. I remained optimistic that his love and dedication to Vinny and Molly's well-being would help carry him through the dark and difficult times.

As Nic and I drove back down the mountain where he would drop me back at my parents' condo, we were quiet. I could tell that he was also experiencing the bittersweetness of a wonderful time with me. The gravity of the unknown of when we would be able to spend this kind of time together again hung heavy in the air.

Our lives in Fargo may not allow for the kind of freedom we just had within the last 20 hours. Nic and I certainly made the best of that time. Nic pulled up to the front door of the condo and hopped out to retrieve my backpack from the back of the 4Runner. We embraced one last time, and he pulled me away from him to look me in the eyes.

"Until our next adventure, sweet Sylvia," Nic said, eyes glistening. "Peace on your journey. See you on the other side." I smiled and kissed him on the cheek and went inside.

***

My mom met me in the lobby looking pale as a ghost.

"Mom?" I asked worriedly. "Are you OK? Are the kids OK? Where's Dad?"

"Sylvia, sit down," she said with authority. I immediately did what she said.

"I have some bad news," she said, tears springing to her eyes.

"Karen called me this morning when she couldn't get ahold of you. It's Andy. Cameron found him this morning in your house. He must have relapsed with alcohol. They think it was acute alcohol poisoning. His system wasn't accustomed to how much he was drinking after having been sober." My mom leaned in toward me and grasped both my hands.

The room was spinning and I felt like I was floating outside my body. Tears started streaming down my mom's face. "I'm so sorry, Sylvia. He didn't make it. The emergency workers tried to revive him, but he's gone. He was pronounced dead at 10 AM this morning."

I stared blankly at her. Through her. "Where are the kids?" I asked flatly. "Do they know?" It was currently 11 AM in Steamboat and noon in Fargo, so my mom must have recently learned this.

"No," she shook her head. "Your dad took them down to the pool. We wanted you to be able to tell them. Sylvia, I'm so sorry. I know your phone wasn't working up in the mountains so you shut it off. You may want to turn it back on now to see if there are any messages."

I stood. "Mom, can you take my backpack to your condo? I want to talk to the kids on my own. I'll go get them from the pool," Mom nodded.

"I'm so sorry, Sylvia. Please don't think this is your fault. Andy was sick and this is a terrible disease. Please don't blame yourself."

"Thanks," I said. "I've got to focus on the kids," I said flatly. I felt numb as I went through the motions of walking toward the pool. I felt like I was in someone else's body. This was a dream, and must be happening to someone else.

186

I had to tell my children their father was dead.

Chapter 36

I greeted the kids and my dad in the pool. I asked them to get out so we could get some lunch. The children didn't seem to think anything was wrong. Molly and Vinny were happy to see me and stories came spilling out of them.

Vinny shared that they went moonlight sledding last night for three hours. Molly added that sledding came after they'd gone to the movies with their grandparents. I nodded and tried to smile and sound excited for my kids' energy and happiness. Their lives would change irreparably soon.

Once the kids and I were back in the condo, I asked them to get changed while I made them lunch. In the kitchen, I reunited with my parents. My dad immediately opened his arms and embraced me in a big bear hug.

"I'm so sorry, Sylvia," he said, voice shaking. "Andy's demons were just too big. I know he tried to help himself so he could be with his family, but his disease got the best of him."

"Thanks," I said, pulling away from his embrace. I had to hold it together long enough to make turkey and cheese sandwiches, and apples and carrots for the kids.

"What can we do to help, Sylvia?" My mom asked. She looked so small and uncertain which was so different from her usual confident self.

"Don't leave me," I said, sounding like a scared little girl. "Can you stay in the room while I tell the kids?" They both nodded.

We heard the kids' feet clomp toward the kitchen and their chitter chatter with one another. So innocent they both were.

"Mom, can I have chocolate milk with lunch?" Molly asked. "Since we're on vacation, it's special," she added trying to justify her request. "Yeah, can I have chocolate milk, too?" Vinny chimed in behind her.

"Of course," I said. We all sat down together and ate our simple lunches. It took every fiber in my being to choke down the food as I had no desire to eat. Everything tasted like cardboard and had the texture to match.

The kids continued to share stories about their sledding adventure and the latest Disney movie they got to see and all the popcorn and licorice they had. They looked at me as if they were testing to see how I'd react to their junk food time with their grandparents. Their nutritional balance was the least of my parenting concerns at the moment.

Once the kids finished their meals, I asked them to join me, and their grandma and grandpa, in the living room for an important family meeting. We settled into the couches and chairs, and I took a deep breath and uttered the most difficult words of my entire life.

"I have some sad news to share with you two," I said, with one arm around each of my children, both of them cuddled in close to me.

"It's about your dad," I paused. "He died." Both children pushed back away from me to look at me in sheer horror.

"That's a lie," Vinny said, tears welling in his eyes.

"That's not a funny joke, Mommy!" Molly said, frowning at me.

"I'm so sorry," I said, soldiering on with what I needed to say to them so they could know the truth. There was no sugarcoating any of this nightmare. "Daddy's friend Cameron went to check on him this morning. He couldn't wake him up, so he called emergency workers to try to help. They did everything they could to help him, but he died."

I could barely get the words out over the huge lump that had formed in my throat making me sound like a frog croaking out the words.

"Why couldn't they wake him up?" Vinny asked. "Was it like the time I couldn't wake up Dad? And then he had to go live with Cameron so he could get better from too much alcohol?"

I nodded. "Yes, very similar," I was relieved that Vinny had an idea of what the situation was like so it didn't feel like important people in your life just up and die for no reason at all.

"He had gone a long time without having alcohol and then his disease got the best of him. He had too much alcohol last night," I confirmed.

I wondered how much I should share with them and still preserve the sanctity of his memory. I pressed on with the facts. My children deserve to know the truth that good people just like their dad struggled. Sometimes, there was nothing anyone could do to help.

"Alcohol can be poisonous when the amount consumed is too much in too short of a time period," I said. "And when Daddy fell asleep, the poison built up in his body. His body wasn't used to that much alcohol in his system. It was too much for his brain, and heart, and lungs, and stomach, and kidneys, and liver to handle all at once."

It was quiet in the room. I didn't fill the space with any more words. I let the truth be heavy in the room. My parents were across the room in their chairs, tears quietly streaming down their faces.

"Mommy?" Molly broke the silence. "Is there anything we could have done if we were there with him?" My heart sank. She named the guilt I felt for not being with Andy when he was going through this. Instead, I was many states away having fun on an adventure.

I answered her honestly. "Maybe," I said. "This is one of the most difficult things about alcohol addiction as a disease. We could have given Daddy all the tools to help him get better. But, he's also human and an adult. In the end, even though he loved all of us so much, his disease overcame him and took him out of our lives way too early."

I had no idea if this would help her. My hope as a mother was that the kids didn't feel guilty about not being able to save their father from his self-destructive path that ultimately took his life.

"Is he at peace now? Can he rest?" Vinny asked.

I wasn't ready for that question. I had no idea how to answer. We weren't practicing Christians, so I wasn't about to tell Vinny that he was in heaven or with the angels as he didn't have the context to understand that.

"Vinny, do you remember where you were before you were born?" I returned his question with a question.

"No," he answered honestly.

"Sometimes I think of the places we go after we die like that," I continued. "It isn't defined because we can't remember it. I think Daddy will show up when we enjoy beautiful sunrises and sunsets. You'll feel him when you two have a great game, or a wonderful birthday. He'll stay with you in your heart, and in your mind, and in your good and bad times. You will carry him with you always. You just won't be able to hug him or talk to him in real life any longer."

"Mommy, I want to go home and hug Grandma Karen and Grandpa Kenny," Molly said. "They must be so sad. Now both Aunt Carrie and Daddy died. They don't have any kids left to hug."

I nodded, finally letting myself begin to cry. I gathered the kids close to me and agreed.

"We'll all fly home tomorrow and you'll have all four of your grandparents to hug," I said. "The Wilde family has to stick close together, OK?" I asked for their agreement. "This is the hardest thing we'll have to do together. Can we all agree to that?"

Chapter 37

The flight back to Fargo from Denver on Sunday morning was a somber one. The kids insisted on sleeping in my bed with me at the hotel on Saturday night. My parents were flying back to Fargo on Monday so I trekked from Steamboat to Denver with them in caravan so they could be with us. Even though given the opportunity to ride with their grandparents, the kids weren't letting me out of their sight. I knew they felt vulnerable and so did I. I didn't mind their warm bodies next to mine, giving me the security and motivation I needed to keep moving forward in the hard days ahead.

Karen and Kenny met us at the Fargo airport. The kids ran to them at baggage claim. They looked stricken. I could not imagine what kind of trauma this brought up for them having both their children die young and tragically.

"I missed you so much," Karen said softly as she stroked Molly's hair, and hugged her tightly. Meanwhile, Kenny, who was not usually overly affectionate, was holding on to Vinny. "We're going through tough times, buddy," he said while hugging Vinny.

Karen turned to me. "Sylvia, I need to say this to you, and you will not interrupt me," I nodded, following her instructions.

"There's nothing you could have done to stop this," she said insistently, grabbing my shoulders. "Andy was our star boy and the light of our lives, but he had this disease and that was more powerful."

Tears were streaming down Karen's face.

"The last few months spent with you and the kids have been healing for Kenny and I. We couldn't save Andy, but we sure as hell aren't losing you and the kids," she added.

I wrapped my arms around my mother-in-law, and let out a little sob.

"I'm so sorry," I said, pulling Kenny into my embrace with Karen. "I didn't think he was this bad," I admitted guiltily. "I thought he was doing so well, and any little relapse was a stumbling block."

Karen nodded. "Believe me, Syl, you'll drive yourself crazy trying to come up with the reasons why, and the things you could have done to stop it. It will get you nowhere."

Kenny nodded in agreement. "Karen and I lost years of our quality of life, and our connection with Andy, blaming ourselves for Carrie's death," Kenny added. "This is awful and I wouldn't wish this on anyone. This time, instead of running away and hiding like we did with Carrie's death, we're going to go through the terrible times together."

As we headed out to the car with our luggage, I felt foolish for asking, but needed to get answers.

"Where did they take him?" I asked after the kids were in the car, but Karen and Kenny and I hadn't gotten in yet. Karen looked at me. "It was an unattended death so they sent him to the medical examiner's office for an autopsy," I nodded. "They told me on the phone that it will be the middle of the week when they return his body to the funeral home. We can still plan to hold a funeral next weekend for him. We should start planning the service tomorrow."

"OK," I said. "Can you please stay with me?" I sounded like a little kid. It was humbling to go from the top of my confidence game a day ago to leaning heavily on my parents and in-laws.

"Of course," Karen said, hugging and comforting me. "I hope your parents will stay, too."

I knew my parents would, and I knew that I would need all the help I could get. There would be arrangements to make. Most important, however, was ensuring the kids had all the love and support they needed.

Then it hit me: Cameron. I couldn't imagine what he was going through. I still hadn't turned on my cell phone as I honestly was not emotionally prepared for what kind of messages might have been left for me while I was in Steamboat.

"Can you drop me off at Cameron's house and take the kids to get settled in at home, please?" I asked.

"Yes, I think that's a good idea," Kenny said. "We haven't had much time to talk to Cam. He's probably feeling pretty rough having found Andy the way he did. He tried so hard to get Andy on a better path."

The Wildes drove me to Cameron's house. I walked up the front steps and knocked on the door. I didn't call so he wasn't expecting me but he answered immediately. His eyes were bloodshot from crying. I rushed into his arms for a hug. We went inside and sat on his couch.

"Cameron, I'm so sorry," I let my tears flow and sank into the strength of his body enveloping me.

"I asked you to help him and then you end up having to be the one to find him," I sobbed.

I felt so guilty that I'd dragged Cam into our shit show of the last two months of Andy's existence.

"Syl, I'm lucky," Cam said. "I got to be with Andy and rekindle our friendship in the best kind of way these last two months," he admitted.

"I didn't tell you this before, but Eleanor and I have been separated since last fall."

I was shocked. They were such an awesome couple. I was questioning now if any relationship had the ability to survive.

"Cam, I'm so sorry," I said. He shrugged.

"She had become increasingly more distant and disconnected from me. When I called her out on it, she admitted she'd been in a relationship for the last few years with a man she'd met on tour while in New York. We tried to make amends, but it's clear that she's in love with him and not the fun-loving, playful, parks guy anymore," Cam added trying to lighten the mood.

"Anyway, I'm telling you this because spending time with Andy gave me a sense of purpose and reignited parts of myself that had been quiet for many years," Cam wiped tears away.

"To be honest, the holidays were really tough for me and I almost relapsed," he looked me in the eyes. "Your call to me asking for help with Andy was the saving grace I needed to keep myself on track. Thank you for that. I can never repay you."

"What was it like?" I pleaded for details. I had no idea what Andy's last two months of life were like. Other than the tidbits I received on Valentine's Day and the coffee shop meet-up a few days before I left for Colorado, I was in the dark.

Cam smiled. "It was rough in the beginning, great in the middle, and rough in the end," Cam reminisced.

"He was in a pretty bad way the first week while detoxing, and starting therapy, and antidepressants. There was a lot to work through with Carrie's death. He blamed himself for letting you and the kids down." Cam stood and started to walk toward the kitchen.

"I'm getting hungry, come with me." I stood and followed him, grateful to not make a decision and be told what to do.

I watched as Cam prepared ground turkey meatballs stuffed with mozzarella with broccoli on the side. As he moved about the kitchen, I appreciated his stories of how many nights were spent after work making dinner together with Andy. Then they would read, relax, and head to bed early.

Cam said that Andy talked about me and the kids a lot. He was sorry for letting himself go so far down the path of addiction. Cam also shared how proud Andy was of my weight loss and wellness journey. He admitted what a jerk he had been to me about it. He was scared that if I lived in a strong, powerful body, there would be no need for him. He thought I would leave him because he was so broken.

I buried my face in my hands and began to cry again. Cam came from behind the kitchen island and took me back in his arms.

"Syl, you've always been strong and powerful in body and mind," Cam said. "You lost sight of that for awhile. When Andy realized that you'd rediscovered this power within you, he knew he was in trouble."

"He didn't say any of these things to me!" I was livid.

I had no idea how scared Andy was feeling. He had been ignoring me for the last six months of our relationship before I asked him to stay with Cam.

"He wasn't in a good place, Syl," Cam continued. "And you kept getting better and better without him. He didn't have the tools to cope."

Cam went on to say that Andy was making great strides in therapy, acknowledging the pain from his sister's death. He was working on the forgiveness process with his parents. Cam shifted uncomfortably as if he wanted to say more but was uncertain if he should.

My eyes narrowed. "Cam, out with it. You cannot keep anything from me. Please, I beg you."

"He made amends with his parents," Cam said. "He'd talk to them over the noon hour each day and meet up with them once or twice a week for lunch. He wanted to keep up with how you and the kids were doing. He swore them to secrecy, but I want you to know that he was so proud of you. He loved hearing about the kids and their stories. He was in a really good place with Kenny and Karen."

My heart soared. I was so glad Andy did that and did not care at all. I would have encouraged it but I assumed Andy wouldn't have listened to me. I'd nagged him in the past to talk to his parents about Carrie and the hurts from his childhood to no avail.

"One more thing," Cam added. "Andy spent last weekend at the house with Kenny and Karen and the kids while you and Roxy went swimsuit shopping in Minneapolis." I smiled. I'd suspected something was up when I returned from my girls trip last weekend. I decided not to press the issue as everyone seemed happy with whatever adventure had played out while I was away.

"Well that's just fabulous," I thanked Cam profusely as we ate our meal together. It was wonderful and I realized I hadn't eaten much over the last few meals. I was so grateful for my tribe and their willingness to take care of me and the kids.

"Can I ask you a question, Syl?" Cam asked timidly as we were washing the dishes together. "Sure," I responded apprehensively.

"Andy was pretty off the rails on Friday night. He called me around 11 PM. He wasn't making much sense. It was clear to me he was drinking," Cam recalled. "I told him he should go to bed. I figured we could deal with his relapse with alcohol in the morning. I asked him to forgive himself for falling off the wagon. But there is one thing he kept saying over and over again that is bugging me. I chalked it up to the repetitive nature that drunks get when they're in the bag."

"What was he saying?" I asked Cam insistently, imploring him for information that would help me piece together Andy's last night on Earth.

"Niksclose," Cam said. "I don't know what that means. But he kept saying that. Do you know what he would have meant by that?"

My heart sank. It was the last conversation he had with me. The fact that there were men's clothes that he'd found in our house. But I didn't and he didn't admit knowing the owner of the clothes. Now I understood he knew who I had been with on Valentine's Day.

He died knowing I'd been unfaithful to him with Nic.

Andy was right.

The men's clothes he'd discovered in our home were indeed, "Nic's clothes."

Chapter 38

Roxy laid with me in my bed on Monday night after she finished work and held me as I cried in her arms. She reassured me that Anna, our boss, was very understanding of the tragedy that occurred with Andy. She insisted I take two weeks off. She told me that everyone at FSG had donated some of their time off. I wouldn't need to dip into any of my time off accrual.

She also told Roxy to tell me that they would delay my job transition so I could take the time I needed. This was such a generous extension of unexpected kindness from my work family. I could barely find the words to show my gratitude.

Roxy stroked my hair and reassured me with her presence and love. After I felt empty from crying, I propped myself up on my elbow to look her in the eyes.

"I have to tell you something and I hope you won't think badly of me," I was worried that if I revealed this shortcoming, Roxy would be so disappointed in me that she'd reconsider her friendship with me.

"Nothing you tell me will make me go away, Sylvia," Roxy said softly. For such a large and commanding presence Roxy had, she was so incredibly gentle with a calm, protective demeanor.

I took a deep breath, gathering courage to share.

"Remember when I met Andy on Valentine's Day in the blizzard to talk at the Indian restaurant?" I began. "Well that night, I left the restaurant before we ordered. Instead, I got stuck on the way home. It happened to be on Nic's street, so he came to get me in his truck. There was no way I was getting home in that weather so I stayed with him," Roxy frowned a bit but didn't interrupt.

"We didn't have sex that night but we were intimate," I admitted. "It felt so good, Rox."

I paused to see if she needed to say anything. I hadn't revealed the nature of my relationship with Nic to her when she and I went on our girl's trip to Minneapolis. I thought she may have felt betrayed that I'd kept this from her.

"He and I also spent time together in Colorado," I continued. "This time, much more romantically and intimately," I said, feeling my cheeks fill with a rush of warmth and comfort with the retelling of our time together.

"Roxy, I was with Nic the night Andy died." My tears began to fall again as I felt shame rise within me.

After letting my tears subside, Roxy finally spoke.

"You didn't know, did you?" Roxy asked softly.

"Know what?" I asked, confused.

"Nic's had feelings for you for years, Syl," Roxy said and I felt my heart skip a beat. My thoughts shifted frantically, combing through my archives of long-term memory looking for evidence of this truth.

"What are you talking about? No he hasn't," I insisted, defensively.

"He and I were both married and I was mostly big and depressed for the years I've known him," I retorted, not willing to acknowledge her revelation to me. This is not the direction I'd intended or predicted this conversation to go at all.

"None of that matters, Syl," Roxy continued, unfazed by my reaction. "Why do you think Anna's been so pissed, threatened, and intimidated by you?" I thought for a moment but didn't respond.

"She likes Nic but none of her feminine wiles work on him. He's so deeply connected to your incredible personality and passion."

This was all very confusing to me.

"Rox, did he talk to you about this?" I felt suspicious that everyone was in on a secret but I was the last to know.

Roxy let out a laugh. "You can be so naive, Syl! It's obvious when spending time with you two the incredible chemistry you have together."

Molly came bursting into the room and jumped on the bed to cuddle between Roxy and I.

"Auntie Roxy are you making Mommy feel better?" Molly asked while snuggling into Roxy.

Vinny came in shortly after Molly, shoulders drooping. He crawled into bed next to me. Vinny didn't often snuggle with me anymore unless he was under the weather. Even though I hated the circumstances, I loved gathering up my not-so-little boy in my arms.

"We're all making your mom feel better, Molly," Roxy said and pressed Molly into the air with her feet so she could pretend to fly like Superwoman. Molly giggled and laughed. I followed suit by pressing Vinny into the air with my feet so he could fly like Superman.

Karen poked her head in the door of the bedroom.

"Sylvia, there's someone here to see you," Karen said. "A man named Dominic."

Roxy looked over at me and raised her eyebrows.

"OK kids, Auntie Roxy is going to take you out for dinner. You both have to eat fruit and veggies. You have to put good fuel in your bodies to grow up strong and capable!"

Roxy scooped up the kids like sacks of flour and went out of the room past Karen who appeared frightened of Roxy's large presence and personality.

"Thanks, Karen," I said. "I'm going to go for a drive with Dominic," I added. "I'll be back a little later." Karen nodded but I could feel her eyes following me suspiciously as I put on my winter gear and headed out the door.

Chapter 39

I hopped into Nic's truck and told him to drive me to his house. He nodded. We drove to his house in silence. When he pulled into his garage and shut the truck off, he broke the silence.

"How do you need me to show up for you right now, Syl?" Nic asked turning toward me. "I am so sorry for your and the kids' loss of Andy. I'm not sure how I can support you. I will do what you tell me to do and try my best to do a good job," Nic said softly.

He was so sweet. He had walked into the dumpster fire of my life that seemed to be getting worse by all accounts. And still, he was willing to ask how best he could help me.

"I don't know, Nic," I said looking at my hands. "Will you please make love to me? I don't want to think about all the things I have to do next and all the decisions I have to make."

"I will gladly do that," Nic said, leaning in and kissing me deeply.

We went into his house and up to his bedroom. The same on which I had slept soundly cuddled up next to him a few weeks before. He slowly undressed me and laid me down on his bed. He then undressed himself.

Even though I felt a deep sadness, I allowed myself to appreciate this moment and this man with his gentle, strong, and kind presence. Nic was patient and made love to me slowly. He gave me the time and space to wiggle and adjust beneath him to get just the right pressure on my clitoris with him on top of me to allow for deeper pleasure.

Just before I reached climax, I said insistently in his ear, "I'm coming, Nic. Fill me up with you. Flood me." He moaned and I felt the warm wetness of him fill me as we came together.

Nic held me after we made love. I didn't mind the silence. This was a lovely, brief reprieve. I felt a pang of hunger and looked over at Nic's bedside table where the clock read 7:30 PM.

"Can you feed me and then take me home, please?" I asked Nic. He nuzzled into my hair.

"Of course," he said, rolling out of bed and springing into action. I hopped up, too, took a quick shower, and joined him downstairs in the kitchen.

"Fish tacos with spicy slaw!" Nic announced. "It's what I had for dinner a few hours ago, but I'm ready for seconds after going a round with you," Nic winked at me.

I ate two tacos, some spicy rice and beans, and a sparkling water. It was delicious.

"Thank you, Nic," I said. "For everything. You're being wonderful. I appreciate you giving me the support to move through this. I have no idea how to do this."

He walked around the table and held me again.

"I'll be here, Syl," Nic said. "I'm not going anywhere." I buried my head in his chest.

"Can I just stay here and hide out?" I asked.

"Nope. Your kids need you," Nic said, ushering me toward the door. I followed him, thankful to have a moment of direction and an easy task to accomplish: get coat and boots on, and get driven home.

Nic and I drove back home in silence. It wasn't strained, just pleasant to not have to fill space.

"Nic?" I asked turning back to face him before closing the door to his truck. "Will you please come to the funeral with Anna and Roxy and Lin? It would mean the world to me to have you there."

"I'll be there," Nic said and smiled. He then looked over my shoulder. "You better go. Karen is looking at us out the window from the house."

Here we go. I didn't have the energy to explain my relationship with Nic to Karen. On the other hand, I was too tired to lie or keep secrets. I'd have to dig deep for the courage to be honest.

Chapter 40

"Ms. Wilde, where would you like to hold the service?" I was already overwhelmed at the planning session with the funeral director and this was his second question. I'd stayed up half the night retrieving pictures of Andy from his childhood, college years, and our time as a family together. Karen and Kenny had returned home on Tuesday morning abruptly.

The night before, Karen asked me to reveal the nature of my relationship with Nic. I admitted we'd been friends for years, but had taken up romantically in the last few weeks.

She was understandably shocked. She told me that I was an ungrateful woman. She also told me how low it was of me to do that to Andy while he was struggling to work on his sobriety.

I didn't want to fight with her, but also shared that Andy had asked me for a divorce. She wasn't aware of this and ran away to her room crying. Tuesday morning, she knocked on my door at 5:30 AM and said that she and Kenny were headed back to the farm in Dooley.

She said her reason was to get photos and memorabilia of Andy's for the funeral. She promised to meet me Wednesday for the funeral planning meeting. When I got up from bed to hug her goodbye, she turned away and rejected my embrace.

"Um. How about the performing arts center on the Red River?" I asked. We weren't religious, so it seemed ridiculous to hold Andy's service in a place of worship.

"Yes, that will work. There's nothing booked the first Saturday in March. Is that OK? It's just a few days away. Will you have enough time to gather family and friends?" The funeral director asked.

Andy wanted to donate his body to science. Our plan was to have a service, and then have his body sent to the medical school so the medical students could use his body to practice and learn.

"Yes, we'll be able to share details on social media and in the paper to let family and friends know," I said flatly. "Did you get the obituary I sent for Andy?" I asked the funeral director.

Karen shot me a glare. "I didn't get to preview it, Sylvia," she said coldly. I rolled my eyes.

"You'll both get to preview it before we put it up on the funeral home website and in the online version of the newspaper," the funeral director said calmly.

I imagined he had to be a mediator quite often in matters of family and stress. "Now, who will be conducting the service? Will there be any special music?" he asked.

"We have a friend Edith that is an officiant. She and I will put together a service and she will deliver it," I responded before Karen could answer.

"And yes, our friend Eleanor will play piano hymns for the service and also accompany our violinist and singer friends Cora and Damien. They'll do Vince Gill and Amy Grant's "Go Rest High on that Mountain.""

Karen looked at me, eyes wide.

"I love that song, and I know Andy would, too," Karen said softly, tears springing to her eyes. I was throwing her a bone. The song had a basis in Christianity. She was a devout, North Dakotan, stoic Lutheran, so I knew she'd appreciate this.

I leaned over and grabbed her hand. "I know. We're going to get through this, Karen," I kissed her hand and continued to answer questions from the funeral director. Karen didn't have to forgive me for being romantic with Nic. However, she did need to know that I was going to honor the life of my husband in the best way I knew how. As we were wrapping up, I had one more question.

"May I see him?" I asked simply. The funeral director looked at me inquisitively.

"Yes...but he's only wearing the hospital gown provided, not the clothes you brought here today. He isn't in his casket. He's on the table," he responded.

Karen took her hand out of mine, suddenly looking scared. I hadn't discussed seeing Andy today with her. I understood if she didn't join me. I nodded at her, giving her permission to pass.

"Shall I take you now?" I stood up from my chair to follow him, the sound of my heart thumping loudly in my ears. I didn't know if this was the right thing to do. I felt I had to see him before Saturday. I needed to be strong for the kids, and the family and friends on the day of his service. I needed this time to say goodbye to my husband.

"Can you wait for me in the family waiting room for ten minutes?" I asked Karen. She nodded, looking small and scared, eyes darting around. This poor woman. I wouldn't wish outliving children on anyone. I hoped I never outlived my children.

I followed the funeral director down the back stairwell to the embalming room. He led me to a table and pulled the sheet back, revealing my husband. My whole world came to a standstill. Time stopped as I looked at him. Starting at the top of his head and moving all the way down to his feet, I worked to memorize his features as this would be one of my final views of him.

"I'll give you a few minutes with your husband," the funeral director said. "I'll be in an office on the other side of the door if you need anything," he said pointing to the doors we just entered.

I nodded, not looking away from Andy.

I ran my fingers through Andy's thick brown hair like I'd done for nearly two decades. It struck me how peaceful he looked. There wasn't a tightness in the furrowed brow that had often accompanied him in life. I couldn't believe how much Vinny was looking like his dad. The same high cheekbones and nose.

"Andy, I'm so sorry," I said aloud, placing his cold, lifeless hand in mine. "I would give anything for things to not have ended this way."

My tears began to fall as I had my last conversation with my husband. "I will do my best to take care of your children. I will remind them of you as often as I can. They'll never forget you."

I was quiet for a moment, gathering my thoughts. "I never meant to hurt you," I admitted. "I'm sorry you went out of this world in so much pain and anguish. I'm sorry I couldn't save you."

I leaned over and placed my head on my husband's chest for the very last time and wept.

There were so many things that would never be shared between us. What I originally envisioned would be a hiccup in our marriage timeline was now a punctuation mark. It was the end of our chapter together. He'd never see our children graduate high school, go to college, get married, have children of their own, and become a grandfather. All of our timelines were altered irreparably.

With all the strength I could muster, I stood again and readjusted the hospital gown on him where I'd left a wet spot from my tears.

"Goodbye, Andy," I said, and pulled the sheet back up to his neck. "Peace on your journey," I said. I kissed his cheek and covered his face.

Weak in the knees, I turned and left the room where the funeral director was waiting to take me back to Karen in the family waiting room. She jumped up from her chair when she saw me.

"How is he?" She asked insistently and then frowned. "I mean, how does he look?" She leaned in to hug me, realizing I was still crying.

"So young," I said honestly. "And so peaceful," which was also true. "I'll miss him, Karen." She buried her head in my chest and sobbed.

"I just can't, Syl," she said between sobs. "I can't look at him, it'll make it too real. I'm not ready. This is so unfair." She was crying and gasping and I had both of us sit back down. The funeral director returned with a bottle of water and more tissues.

"I'm sorry," Karen said once she calmed her breathing. "I have so much work to do," she admitted. "I haven't properly grieved Carrie, and now I have to say goodbye to my baby boy."

She put her face in her hands and quietly cried as her shoulders bounced lightly up and down. She was trying to hide from this nightmare of motherhood repeated. I reached out and put my hand on her knee.

"Karen, Molly, and Vinny are the luckiest kids on the planet," I said, and I meant it. "The silver lining of this tragedy is that the kids get to keep their father's memory alive with you. There's no way you and Kenny would have come into the kids' lives if Andy hadn't struggled. They need you," I said. "And I need you."

Karen took a deep breath. "I'm exhausted from crying, Syl. Take me home so I can hug my grandbabies," Karen said as she stood.

Chapter 41

"Roxy, nothing fits!" I complained into the phone at 6:30 AM the morning of Andy's funeral.

"We'll figure this out. I'll be over in 20 minutes," Roxy said and we hung up.

I laid on the floor of my closet and cried. After seeing Andy at the funeral home, all of my memories with him flooded into the forefront of my mind. Before seeing his body and truly acknowledging his death, I was able to disassociate. I felt like all of this was happening to someone else.

Going through old pictures of us from high school and college, our wedding, the birth of our children, holiday gatherings, and family vacations left a black hole of emptiness within me. Saying goodbye to Andy today, with family and friends by my side, would prove to be the hardest day of my life.

"Mom, are you here?" Molly and Vinny called from the bed. They'd both taken to sleeping next to me in my bed since their dad died. I had zero problems with this. I needed them as much as they needed me. It was important to keep them close and we gave each other comfort.

They'd asked to go to school when we returned from Colorado and I couldn't believe how incredibly brave that was of them. They seemed to be getting an outpouring of love and support from their friends and teachers. I felt relieved we all had such a large tribe to lean on right now. Our doorbell had been ringing non-stop. There was so much food in the deep freeze and downstairs refrigerator. We'd easily eat all spring and summer.

"Yes, I'm in the closet," I called back to them. "Roxy is coming over to help me find something to wear to the funeral today." They hopped off the bed and joined me in the closet.

"Mom, you have to get rid of all these big clothes," Vinny said. "You're just a medium person now." I gave him a hug. He was right. I was about 212 when I left for Colorado on vacation a week and a half ago. I had likely lost another five to ten pounds over the course of the last week.

I actually made time to steal away to the basement each day since we'd been back. Sweating on the treadmill and lifting heavy weights in the basement felt so good. It gave me a brief respite from all the things out of my control. I was grateful for a habit that allowed me to take care of myself and the kids. It gave me the strength to get through whatever was in store for our family of three.

"Thanks, buddy," I said. "I'll pack these up next week when you two are on spring break from school. You can help me donate all of these things that don't fit me anymore."

"Mommy, am I allowed to hug Daddy when he's dead today?" Molly asked me with big, sad eyes. I pulled her on my lap and hugged her tightly.

"Yes, and you can even give him a kiss on the cheek," I reassured her. "His body will feel stiff and cold because the life has gone out of it. You can certainly lean into his casket and hug him goodbye. I think that would make you feel really good to give your dad a final goodbye hug and kiss." Molly nodded and tears rolled down her cheeks.

"I'm going to miss him so much, Mommy," Molly whispered. "He would play with me in the backyard and cheer so loud for me at gymnastics. Will you please do that for me now?"

I squeezed her tightly. "I might not do things exactly how your dad did, but I will do my best, sweetie."

"I'm mad at Dad," Vinny said, arms crossed at his chest. "He shouldn't have had so much alcohol that he couldn't live. How come he didn't love us enough to want to stay with us?" Vinny was frowning and his voice was cold.

"He loved us so much, Vinny," I responded. "He had a disease that clouded his judgment. I honestly don't think he meant to die. I think he accidentally put too much alcohol in his body. Because he wasn't used to it, his body had a bad reaction to it. This isn't fair and it doesn't make sense and you can be as mad as you need to be."

I wanted him to know that it was healthy to feel upset with his dad. The last thing I wanted to do was make him feel like his feelings were bad or wrong.

"I want to be mad for awhile and not hug people," Vinny admitted. "So many people want to hug me and it makes me mad."

I nodded. "You can always decline if you'd like, Vinny. You teach people how to treat you. Politely let them know that you don't care for a hug right now."

I thought a bit more. "You know what?"

They both looked at me. "We're all going to talk to a counselor that is trained in helping people through really tough times in life. We'll go together the three of us. Then, we'll all go on our own so we can have our own journeys and stories to share. How we grieve for dad is going to be different for each of us." They nodded in agreement.

"Knock, knock," Roxy poked her head into my closet. "Is there room for one more in here?" We laughed as it was getting pretty cramped already with me and the kids in there. The kids jumped up to hug Roxy.

"Come on Molly, let's get some breakfast and start getting ready," Vinny held out his hand to Molly. She took it and they walked out of the room. He was getting so grown up. I didn't want him to have to grow up so quickly. I hoped that the kids could come through this terrible tragedy relatively unscathed.

"I brought a load of clothes," Roxy said pointing to my bed. "I figure you're pretty close to my size now, we can share clothes!" This realization lifted my spirits. Roxy had incredible, funky fresh style. Her personal style informed much of the purchasing I did for our women's clothing line at work.

226

I grabbed a black and silver long-sleeved dress off the pile. I threw it over my bra and underwear. It hit me just above my knees and grabbed my curves.

"What do you think?" I asked Roxy doing a twirl. "Will it work? Is it too flashy for a somber day?"

"It's absolutely stunning," Roxy admired me and ran her hand down the length of my right arm. There was a little bit of shimmer in the silver of the fabric. I sparkled a bit when I moved.

"I think it's OK to have a little shimmer of hope on a sad day. We're supposed to celebrate Andy and his life. We can't be sad sacks the whole time, right?" Roxy asked hopefully.

I smiled. "That's right," I said as I took the dress off. I put my sweatpants and t-shirt back on. It was time to shower, get ready, and face the reality of the day.

"Can you and Lin sit with me and the family today, please?"

"Yes, my dear." Roxy left even though I would have preferred her to stay. I wanted her to hold my hand the whole day. I knew I had to move through this difficulty on my own.

Chapter 42

I heard Eleanor's beautiful piano music when I entered the main hall of the performing arts center. With each of my children's hands in mine, we marched up front to where Andy was in his casket. The kids and I peered into the casket together to admire the husband and father Andy was.

"Hi, Daddy," Molly said, reaching in her hand and placing it on his. "I'll miss you so much. I had so much fun playing soccer in the backyard with you. And when I looked up at gymnastics, you'd always be cheering and smiling. Mommy does OK, but you're the best at roughhousing."

Molly placed a bracelet she'd made in Andy's casket with him. She then asked me to pick her up so she could lean in and give him a hug and a kiss. I did as I was told.

"Goodbye, Daddy. I'm sorry I won't get to play with you and see you anymore," she turned to look at me with tears in her eyes. "Mommy, I want to go sit with my grandmas and grandpas, OK?" she asked.

I turned to look behind me and saw my mom and dad sitting next to Karen and Kenny. They'd always gotten along well. I was glad they'd stuck close to one another today. I put Molly down so she could be with her grandparents.

"Hi, Dad," Vinny said, hands crammed in his pockets. "I'm still really mad at you. I can't believe we won't be able to play football in the neighborhood with the other kids. You'll never get to see me play in any of my games," Vinny said, honestly. "I really hope you can be more at peace now. It made me sad to see you so unhappy. I think you got lost and turned around inside yourself. I just want you to know that even though I'm mad, I forgive you. We're supposed to forgive everyone that makes mistakes."

Vinny leaned in and hugged Andy. "Goodbye, Dad. I promise I'll take really good care of Mom and Molly," Vinny turned around and hugged me. He then went to join Molly and his grandparents.

I stood near Andy's casket as more and more family and friends poured in to pay their respects. My brother Silas and his family arrived next. There was a steady stream of co-workers from both Andy and my jobs. Cameron and the other college football buddies created a large presence in both numbers and physicality.

Roxy, Lin, Nic, and Anna arrived shortly after the football team entourage.

It was incredible to see so many people show up to say goodbye to Andy. I had to numb myself from the outpouring of love from the hugs and condolences offered. I might not get through the service without breaking down if I let myself feel too much. I had to stay strong today.

Nic gave me a big hug when he came by and I said, "Thank you for being here today. It means so much to me."

He smiled and leaned in to whisper in my ear, "You look so beautiful. When your day is done, please come over so I can hold you." I nodded, grateful for the offer.

Andy's funeral service was beautifully delivered. Andy's college football teammates, including Cameron, were all wearing Andy's lucky number seven jersey. They must have had them made. The running joke from the color analyst that called the games back in college was "Seven is Wilde."

The kids and I were flanked by Karen and Kenny on one side, my parents and brother and his family on the other side of us. Roxy and Lin sat behind me and Roxy would reach out and place a hand on my shoulder from time to time. Nic and Anna were seated in the row behind Roxy and Lin. I was fortunate in the amount of support I had in the form of family and friends. It made it all a little more bearable.

After the service, we had a luncheon in the main hall. A slideshow of pictures and video served as the highlight reel of Andy's life. The looped projection of his life served as the backdrop for the meal. By 1 PM, most everyone had left except for the support staff at the venue.

Both sets of parents and my brother and family returned to my house.. I was so bone tired, I felt like I could sleep for a week. I'd never felt such a deep exhaustion. I texted my mom and let her know that I wanted to have a few hours of alone time. I told her I'd be home by dinnertime.

I decided to take Nic up on his offer from earlier. I left the performing arts center after thanking the funeral director for his and his staff's exceptional care.

I didn't call Nic on my way to his house as I figured the offer still stood from that morning. There was a car parked in the driveway when I pulled in so I regretted not giving Nic a heads up about my arrival. Maybe Nic had a buddy over.

I decided to go up the steps and drop in on him anyway. I was stopped dead in my tracks with my finger poised over the doorbell at what I saw. As I squinted in the window next to his door, I could not believe what I was seeing.

It was Anna. She was sitting on the couch leaning over Nic and they were kissing. My blood ran cold. Nic noticed me with my jaw dropped in shock staring back at him. He pushed Anna off him and rushed towards the door. I turned away and strode back to my car, livid.

"Sylvia, wait," Nic said, emerging from his house, and running down the front steps toward me. "It's not what it looks like!" Anna emerged behind Nic looking annoyed.

I spun around. "Sorry to interrupt, Anna," I said flatly, glaring at both of them. "Nic said I was welcome to stop by. I didn't realize he'd made other plans in the meantime." I opened my car door and got in before either of them could respond.

Chapter 43

After spending a week at our house after the funeral, Karen and Kenny, my parents, and Silas and his family left to return to their respective homes. The kids got their things set out for returning to school, and I prepared myself the best I could for my return to work.

I was eternally grateful that I would be starting at our warehouse location which meant that I wouldn't have to face Nic and Anna. If I weren't so tired and empty, I would feel heartbroken and betrayed by what I'd witnessed between Nic and Anna. It was incredibly insulting to know that Nic and Anna had been together on the same day as Andy's funeral.

I did everything in my power to put any of my feelings for Nic completely out of my mind. He'd shown his true colors. It seemed to be in stark contrast to the time Nic and I had in Steamboat. I couldn't control other people's choices, yet I was deeply hurt by Nic and Anna's behavior.

My job now was to double down on my and my children's health and well-being. I needed to have laser focus to guide my children and myself out of the darkness of our loss of Andy. I couldn't be distracted by the trivialities of a lusty fling.

Roxy and Lin continued to be incredibly supportive. Lin taught chemistry classes and labs mornings at NDSU so she agreed to pick up the kids and bring them to her and Roxy's house. That way, I could pick them up when I was done with work at 5:30 PM.

The first few weeks adjusting to our new routine were rocky. Between therapy appointments, after school activities, planning and preparing food, washing and putting away clothes, and keeping the house clean, we were barely getting by.

Nic texted me and called me several times each week, but I never returned his bids for communication. Anna straight-up pretended that nothing had occurred between her and Nic. This was probably advisable from a human resources perspective. I had quite a bit of leverage if I were ever to go to the board of directors with my knowledge of her and Nic's indiscretion. It was between her, as the boss, and Nic, as her direct report.

Roxy came to visit me at my new office at the warehouse during my second week back to work. She offered to take me out to lunch. There was a cute little taco shop next to a hip brewery that just opened. It was late March, and though it still felt like winter in Fargo, the warmth of the sun gave indications of spring.

"Let's get a taco combo so we can try each other's," Roxy insisted. An excellent idea considering there were kimchi and BBQ taco options. This way we didn't have to limit ourselves. "You're looking pretty trim, lady," Roxy said as we were waiting for our food.

"Yeah, I haven't had as much of an appetite these last three weeks," I admitted. I'd been eating meals with the kids, but I think the stress of our lives, and my dependence on exercise as my stress reliever continued my weight loss pattern.

"Have you talked to Nic lately?" Roxy asked. I looked away, somewhat ashamed as I had completely ignored him. Instead of answering her question, I asked one of my own. "Why do you ask?"

"He put in his two-week notice today," Roxy responded. "He took a job at NDSU as an athletic trainer for their football team during the season. He'll also teach physical therapy classes throughout the school year. He says he wants to get back to helping and coaching people instead of selling fitness equipment. He doesn't start the job until July, so he's going to take a few months off and travel and personal train some clients before he starts full-time."

I nodded and sipped my lemonade. I tried to put all my thoughts of Nic out of my head. Even though part of me was proud of the change he was making, I was still pissed that he'd betrayed me by taking up with Anna. I hadn't told Roxy what I witnessed the day of the funeral between Nic and Anna. I knew she'd be mad and a mad Roxy was a bull in a china shop. I feared the verbal lashing she would unleash upon Nic.

"Have you checked your email today?"

I hadn't. I was getting settled and interviewing warehouse staff. I was also getting the workflow organized for orders to flow from the online portal smoothly to shipping and receiving and making sure we had the right quantities of the items we were selling online.

We were going to launch with our summer apparel line first, so even though it was March, we had a ton of swimsuits and beachwear about to go live online. I sure hoped this worked, and the online shopping portal for FSG was successful. If it didn't, I feared I would be out of a job.

"No. Why?" I cocked my head to the side, looking at Roxy suspiciously. She sure was a wealth of work knowledge today.

"Anna is resigning effective April 1," Roxy smiled at me. "It's not an April Fool's joke." I suspected she and Nic wanted to make their relationship more official, so they were both bailing on FSG as to not get in trouble. They likely needed to keep their reputations clean.

"You can read it later but she stated that she'd be looking for a replacement within the company. She felt she wasn't as suited to passionately run the company like her father was. She wants to hire from within to make sure FSG is in good hands. She'll be moving to California."

Just then, our tacos arrived. I didn't even acknowledge the server placing the steaming plates in front of us.

"You OK, Syl?" Roxy asked, diving into a kimchi taco. "Yes, but I'm shocked."

Who would Anna hire? I certainly didn't want that type of responsibility. I was digging my new role in the warehouse. Plus, I wouldn't be able to put in 60 hours of work each week being the only parent to my kids. I really liked my eight to five gig and not having to take work home with me.

"You should do it," I said to Roxy. "What?" Roxy responded, pausing her taco next to her mouth, just before taking her first bite.

"You'd be perfect. You're passionate, you're a strong leader, you're creative, you have a strong sense of justice, and you're disciplined. Please tell me you'll apply for it," I insisted.

For the first time in as long as I could remember, Roxy was silent. I think I surprised her with my recommendation it had rendered her speechless.

"OK," Roxy said, determined. "You convinced me. I'll do it." We finished our taco lunch and I hurried back to my office to fire up my email. I wanted to read Anna's announcement.

I sifted through some of the top priority emails and then an email came through from Anna. The subject was, "We Need To Talk." I felt my cheeks flush. What would she want from me? The body of the email read:

Sylvia,

Let's get together tomorrow afternoon for a meeting. You can update me on the warehouse operations and I can share a few things with you before I'm done on April 1. I need to clear the air with you.

-A

Chapter 44

Anna asked to meet me at the downtown Fargo Library in one of their small meeting rooms. I entertained myself thinking that the reason she called this meeting at a neutral, off-site location was that she might try to shank me to keep me quiet about her indiscretion with Nic.

I smiled to myself thinking of what she might attempt to try to overpower me. I was nearly a foot taller than her and very strong physically. I was also mentally sound since weathering the storm of becoming a widow. I felt prepared to handle whatever attack, physical or verbal, she brought my way.

She stood as I entered the meeting room. She looked scared. It wasn't an emotion I'd ever seen her show. She always exuded confidence. She walked toward me arms open for a hug. I crossed my arms letting her know that I was *definitely* not open to a hug. She awkwardly patted and petted my arm like I might be a feral dog.

"Sylvia, how are you doing?" she asked with what appeared to be genuine concern. I did not trust this woman.

"With what, Anna? The loss of my husband and my children's father? Or with witnessing my boss and coworker making out on the day of my husband's funeral?" I asked her coldly. Her cheeks flushed red and she gestured to a chair for me to sit down.

"That's why I called you here, Sylvia," Anna began. "You likely already know that Nic and I are both leaving FSG on April 1."

"That's convenient, isn't it?" I asked bitterly. "Maybe he'll join you in California for awhile so you can have your boy toy with you until he starts his job with NDSU this summer."

"Sylvia, will you please just listen to me," Anna's eyes were welling up with tears. I sighed loudly, but stayed quiet.

"I've been interested in Nic for a long time and I realize that's inappropriate," she continued. No shit, Sherlock, I thought to myself, considering she was his boss. I crossed my arms and shifted in my chair.

"I've been jealous of you for so long, Sylvia," Anna said. My eyes narrowed at her. Was I being punked? What the hell was she talking about?

"You and Roxy and Nic were always so close at work and I never fit in. And the fact that Nic has always been so in love with you...it just made me resent you so much." I frowned at her.

What was she talking about? I never noticed Nic giving me anything other than friendly attention at work over the years. Now, within the last few weeks, both Roxy and Anna have made it clear that Nic had a thing for me.

"I invited myself over to his house the day of Andy's funeral," Anna admitted. "I called him about an hour after we left the luncheon, and made up an excuse that I wanted to see some of his fitness equipment in his home gym. I told him I wanted to see if we should purchase those same styles and brands for FSG."

She paused.

"He hesitated, and then told me that it would have to be quick. He said he was preparing for company later that day and he wasn't sure when that company would arrive."

Anna paused to look at me and then continued with her confession.

"I doubled down on my flirting efforts as soon as I got in the door and he was having none of it. He shut me down at every turn. He showed me the equipment and then tried to get me to leave. I faked feeling lightheaded and asked for a little ice water and a chance to sit down for a minute on his couch. When he sat down

242

next to me to check and see if I was OK, I moved in on him and started kissing him."

Anna wouldn't meet my gaze, and instead looked down at her hands, ashamedly.

"You were the company, Sylvia," Anna said, and looked up at me. "You're the woman he was waiting for and wanting. You always have been," Anna said, tears rolling down her cheeks. "I'm so sorry, Sylvia," Anna finished.

I unfolded my arms and reached out to hand Anna a few tissues to blow her nose. I wanted to be mad at her, but I knew how she felt. I didn't think it happened to people who looked like Anna, but she'd been rejected and it stung like a fresh wound.

"Until very recently, I had no idea Nic liked me, Anna," I admitted, honestly. Anna laughed. "You know, Sylvia, for an intelligent woman you can be really dense when it comes to picking up on the vibes when someone likes you." I smiled at her.

"Thanks for letting me know, Anna. I forgive you." I had more things I wanted to ask her now that her shield was down. I didn't know how long this openness would last. "Why are you going to California?"

"I cannot do Fargo any longer," Anna admitted. "The winters are too punishing and I think I need 75 degrees and sunny to thrive. I have friends that work in fashion there so I'll find a gig eventually. First I need to find myself because I've been acting like a shitty boss and person lately. This is not how my dad raised me. He would have expected more of me."

"Can I make a recommendation, Anna?" I asked.

"Of course," Anna responded, eager to do what I said to make amends.

"Hire Roxy and make Bob proud." A huge smile spread across her face showing off her perfectly straight and white teeth.

"That is exactly what I was thinking," she said proudly.

We both stood and this time I opened my arms for a hug with her. I was surprised how fragile she seemed. Like a scared, directionless child instead of the harsh, critical boss I'd taken her for in the past. I hoped that the California sun would be exactly what she needed to heal and find her strength again.

"Can I share a piece of advice with you, Anna?" She nodded.

"Don't look for a man to fill your cup. That's up to you. Whomever you find should consider themselves lucky to share space with you. Don't give away your power too easily."

"Thank you, Sylvia, I've always admired you and never had enough confidence to tell you."

"Thanks, Anna. I'm glad you told me."

As I walked out of the library, I plucked my phone out of my purse and called Nic.

Chapter 45

"Hello, Syl?" Nic picked up on the first ring.

"Hey, Nic, I talked to Anna today," I began. "I'm sorry I've been ignoring you."

"Oh, Syl, I should never have let her come over in the first place. It was so stupid. I don't trust her. I'm so sorry, Syl. I never meant for anything like that to happen." Everything that had likely been building up in Nic was spilling out.

"I forgive you, Nic," I said, genuinely. "Have you really been in love with me for awhile?" There was a pause on the other end of the line.

"Well, I obviously didn't share this with you at the time, but when Sarah and I were really rocky in our marriage before ultimately deciding to divorce, I shared that I had feelings for someone at work." My heart started beating faster.

"Syl, I've had a thing for you ever since I first met you." I felt myself getting mad.

"I was 300 pounds!" I yelled into the phone. "You couldn't have had a thing for me then!" I insisted.

"Um, yeah I did," Nic responded, defensively. "You're smart, funny, beautiful, assertive, playful, a wonderful conversationalist, caring, and kind. How could I not be attracted to you?"

I had no idea what to do with this revelation. It was easier if Nic could just follow the script I'd played in my head. It went like this: I was a big girl that was fun for a night, or weekend. In the end, the big girl was always going to get passed over for the cute, small blonde with great legs and big boobs. This is what society wanted to see and I believed it, too.

"Sylvia? Are you there?" I sniffed.

"Yes, just rewriting the narrative in my mind of what I knew the nature of your and my relationship to be," I said softly.

"Nic, this isn't going to be easy. I'm not going to be able to be light-hearted and fun, and carefree, and happy-go-lucky. I'm dealing with some heavy shit in my life. I have to help walk my kids through this. I don't know what to say," I admitted.

"I'm a patient man, Sylvia," Nic said. "Just don't shut me out. Let me in. Be vulnerable with me. I'm not going to push you into a serious relationship with me. But I do want to be here for you. You decide how much or how little you see me. You call the shots."

"You can't rescue me," I said, sternly.

"I wouldn't dream of it," Nic responded quickly. "Plus, you don't need any rescuing. You're doing great rescuing yourself."

"Nic, congratulations on your new job," I said, excitedly, knowing that my friend and lover was in my corner with me.

"Thanks, babe," Nic said, with a smile in his voice. "I hope to see you soon."

Chapter 46

"Mom! Wake up! It's the last day of school! You have to walk me to my last day of first grade!" Molly said, shaking me and then standing up to jump on the bed. Vinny came in behind her and had his own demands.

"Mom, let's bike instead. It's so nice outside and I already made pancakes for us so we can eat quickly and then get the bikes out!"

"OK, you convinced me!" I said, excitedly throwing off the covers and tickling the kids until they begged me to stop.

"Let me hop in the shower and get ready for work because I'll bike there, too."

Vinny smiled at me. "Yeah, because you have to get ready for your first race!"

I recently signed up for my first Half Ironman distance triathlon. I'd been swimming and biking in addition to my running and lifting training. My race was in September and Roxy was going to compete with me in Custer, South Dakota.

Nic was coming as well, but as a cheerleader and coach. He'd gotten a substitute for his athletic training gig as the event was during NDSU's first home football game of the season. I'd taken Nic on as my informal triathlon coach. He had so many years of experience it'd be foolish not to work with him. He was encouraging, but with an edge to push me. It was a way we could spend time together several times a week, but without too much pressure on us and our relationship. The sex and intimacy between us continued to vacillate between slow burn and fireworks. We had so much friendship history as our foundation, our mutual respect for one another allowed us to be free and open with one another in bed.

We mostly got to enjoy moving our bodies together getting me ready for my first Half Ironman. We were going to do a shorter distance triathlon in July, and a little longer distance in August to get me ready.

I enjoyed training with Nic, but I also relished going on long runs with Roxy when she could fit them in her schedule. She absolutely rocked her Grand Canyon Ultra Marathon earlier in the month. It was a delight to surprise her, and cheer her on with Nic and Lin.

Lin was still picking up the kids to have them at her house until I picked them up after work. The kids loved spending time with

Lin and the feeling was mutual. Not that she would admit it, but I think Lin enjoyed the company of Vinny and Molly. Lin missed Roxy. Roxy's job was keeping her away from home more than Lin liked but she was proud of her wife and fully supportive.

Roxy's new role as CEO of FSG kept her incredibly busy. Roxy brought all of her amazing talents into her leadership role and was absolutely rocking it. She wasn't afraid to speak her mind, and encouraged her staff, myself included, to push themselves. Together, we all produced high-quality work and stretched the boundaries of what we thought possible.

I also enjoyed training on my own. On long bike rides, runs, and swims, I could think about Andy, our past together, and honor his memory. We put a bench in our backyard and whenever Molly, Vinny or I were having a "Bad Dad Day" we'd go sit on the bench. It was our place to think about him, and talk to him aloud or in our minds.

It really seemed to help in between our therapy sessions to have that place to go with our grief and anger. We'd already joked that we'd have to bring the bench inside to the basement during the winter. We definitely weren't going to go sit in the backyard at the reflection spot when it was -40 degrees and blizzardy. It just showed the kids and I how literally inconvenient the grief process can be.

When we arrived at school on our bikes, both Molly and Vinny's teachers were outside welcoming the kids to school on their last day. Molly's teacher, Ms. Sanderson, clapped and whooped when she saw us. There was pop music pumping out of the loudspeakers. The teachers made a big deal of the last day before summer vacation with games, treats, and activities to celebrate the kids.

"Oh my goodness, Ms. Wilde, you look fabulous! So strong!" Ms. Sanderson said, just as excited to see me as she was to see the kids.

"Thank you!" I beamed. I worked really hard this past year. The additional stress from Andy's death caused me to drop weight really quickly in March and April. This past month, I'd added in a consistent weightlifting routine to make me feel stronger in my changing body.

"Good luck on your races this summer and fall; Molly talks about how strong you are all the time!" Ms. Sanderson high-fived me along with the children. Molly smiled up at me. There was nothing I'd found that was more motivating than the pride my children had lovingly directed toward me.

Even though they'd lost so much, they didn't turn away from me. We'd continue to be the strongest trifecta possible as we moved through the years together: the Wilde bunch.

Vinny spotted his third grade teacher, Mr. Bellanger, and waved wildly. He was excited to have made it to this point in his seniority. All the kids in kindergarten through third grade had lined up and cheered the fourth graders into the school at the beginning of the day. They did the same at the end of the day, leading them out of their elementary career, into their middle school years. Vinny was so excited to be a big fourth grader next fall!

"How've you been, Ms. Wilde?" Mr. Bellanger asked with genuine concern. I nodded, and gave him a smile.

"We're taking it day by day," I answered, honestly. "We try not to set really high expectations for one another in our house. We never know when our grief will hit and derail us."

The kids had the opportunity to meet twice a week for 30 minutes with the school counselor ever since their dad died. Along with the individual and family counseling we did outside of the school day, I felt I was setting them up with the emotional tools and skills to move through their grief.

"Well, I've sure seen an incredible change in Vinny these last few months," Mr. Bellanger admitted. "He's the first to rush in and stick up for someone, or go to them when they're hurt or upset," he said. "He was more guarded and shy at the beginning of the school year, but now I see him really growing into a nurturing and caring young man."

I felt tears well in my eyes. That was such an incredible compliment to hear about Vinny. I worried that he'd go stone cold and distant on me. Or worse, think he had to be the "man" of the house now that his dad was gone. Instead, he was showing his softer, more vulnerable side. He had such a great love of football, and sports of all sorts, that I hoped he wouldn't let that be the only thing that defined him. I breathed a sigh of relief.

I hugged the kids, and biked the four miles to work feeling a sense of relief. I carried so much worry and concern for the well-being of my children through this tragedy. I hadn't noticed how incredibly resilient they were. We were going to be OK.

Chapter 47

I arrived at Cameron's house at 11 AM one sunny, Saturday morning in early June after a long training run. I'd been putting off this task all spring but felt I was in a good place emotionally to move through this dreaded step in the process. Our plan was to go through the things that Andy had kept in Cameron's guest bedroom when he stayed with him.

"Are you ready for this?" Cameron said, as he answered the door freshly showered. He'd, no doubt, just gotten a workout in as well. "Do you want a cup of coffee first?" I shook my head, 'No.'

"Better to just rip off the Band-Aid, Cam," I said. "You've been generous enough to hold on to these things through winter and spring. I need to do this while my mindset is feeling strong."

We headed up to the bedroom. When Cam opened the door, I felt like I'd been kicked in the gut. Andy's scent wafted out of the room. I'd gotten him Calvin Klein *Eternity* cologne as one of the first gifts when we first began dating in high school.

He never stopped using it. He said it was "Sylvia's scent." He said if he stopped wearing it, I might not be able to sniff him out and make my way back to him. The memory shattered my heart into a million pieces, while at the same time made me let out a high-pitched giggle.

"Are you OK?" Cameron asked, trying to discern whether I was about to laugh, or cry hysterically.

"Yeah," I assured him. "Do you mind if I have a few moments alone with Andy's things?" I asked. "I'll call down to you if I need anything." He obliged and closed the door behind him.

I sat down on the bed and looked around surveying the space for clues as to what made up the last few months of his life. A life I was largely no longer a part of, unfortunately. I felt a deep sense of guilt and exhaustion and laid down on Andy's pillow. I don't know if it was possible this many months later, but his pillow smelled like him. Not necessarily his cologne or body wash, just his special blend of scent that I'd grown so accustomed to over the years. It was my normal, my safety, my security.

I began to cry. I felt mad, and frustrated, and cheated out of closure. I would never be able to talk through things with him to reach a resolution. This seemed like the longest, stupidest cliffhanger. But, I had no choice but to live with it for the rest of my life. The guilt of this felt heavy as lead within me. Before this powerful feeling overtook me, I sat up and reached into one of the boxes of Andy's things that Cam had packed up.

There were pictures of the kids, our family, and Andy's football days. I lifted his cherished game ball from a championship win signed by all his teammates and the coach from his senior year in college. There were a few Lego mini figures of superheroes, and at the bottom of the box, a t-shirt. I grabbed the t-shirt to separate it into the clothes pile but it was wrapping something, acting as a cotton sheath.

I pulled at it, and it released a spiral bound notebook. My heart began beating faster. The front cover said, "Andy's Lame Ass Attempt at Journaling to Get Sober and Save My Family." I smiled. I paused for a moment, wondering if I should read his personal words. I quickly decided that I'd spent plenty of time yearning for resolution. If the answers were within these pages, I needed to know.

I flipped open to the first pages, laid back in the bed, and began reading.

He shared how guilty and sad he was in early January for messing up his life this badly. He went on to write about how embarrassed he was to have let himself go. He was sorry for having made Vinny so frightened the day he found him passed out in bed last December. He was sorry to have let me down.

I had to tell myself to breathe as I scanned his words. He journaled through his several relapses. He wrote about how happy he was that Cam had treated him with kindness. He also shared that Cam was such a hard ass about eating right and working out but there was nowhere to hide from him because he was living in his house. I smiled. When Cam was serious about a workout or a meal, he was all in, and everyone in his vicinity better be, too.

I flipped to February 15. The day after our Valentine's meal. Andy wrote how disappointed he was in himself. He wrote that he shouldn't have pushed me to accept him back at home, but he was so desperate to be back with me and the kids. He went on to admit how mad he was at himself for not being supportive of me as I embarked on my health and wellness journey.

He wrote about how incredibly proud he was of me but he was in such a rotten place he couldn't admit how impressed he was with my grit and resilience. I sighed. He really was trying so hard. I wondered if I'd been too harsh in holding my boundaries as he worked toward sobriety.

I turned to a journal entry dated February 21.

Sylvia is going to be out of town and I'm going to stay at the
house. I feel like this is it. This is going to be the only chance
I get to make it right with her and the kids. I plan to do all
the little honey-do fix it things I've put off for years. Paint the
interior, deep-clean, everything I can in the five days she's
gone. She looks gorgeous and fit and seems so happy. I hope
she'll have me. I love her and the kids more than anything in
the whole world and I'll do whatever it takes to make my
family whole again.

That was the last journal entry. Andy likely found Nic's
clothes at the house the next day, went on a two day alcohol-fueled
bender, and died.

Chapter 48

I descended the stairs carrying the two boxes of Andy's personal items and clothes, with his pillow on top. When Cam noticed my load, he ran over to try to help me.

"I've got it," I said. "Will you please open the door and open my car door to the back seat so I can put this in there?" Cam rushed ahead of me opening the doors I requested.

When we returned inside, Cam had prepared us lunch so I sat and ate with him. I was grateful for the time to debrief and my run earlier made me hungry for a good meal.

"How did it go?" Cam asked as we ate our beet salads with rotisserie shredded chicken and fresh bread outside on the deck. It tasted divine.

"Firstly, Cam, this food is amazing," I said. "Exactly what my body is craving after the long run and so light and fresh for summer!" Cam blushed, and I could tell he enjoyed my compliment.

"I've been getting more creative in the kitchen on my own this past fall and winter. I used to cook out of packages when Eleanor was on tour. Now, I'm taking the time to create things from scratch," he said proudly.

Then, he looked down at his plate and pushed a beet around with his fork like it was a hockey puck looking for a goal. "Eleanor and my divorce was final on May 15."

"Oh Cam, I'm so sorry," I said, and reached out and put my hand on top of his forearm. It was strong and muscular. He placed his hand on top of mine.

"Thanks, Syl," he said. "I really do want to hear how it went going through Andy's things," he said, turning the conversation back to me. We returned to eating our salads as I thought how best to describe what had just happened upstairs.

"I keep going back and forth, Cam, about how I miss him, how guilty I feel, and how pissed I am at him for dying," I shared honestly.

"The scent of his cologne takes me back to being 17 and in love with him with a bright future ahead. He had a journal he was keeping. It showed how hard he was working toward his sobriety and how much he wanted to come home and have a fresh start." Cam nodded in agreement.

"Can you tell me what it was like when he was here with you?" I asked, desperately trying to piece together what those last months were like for Andy on a day to day basis.

"Well, it felt like college again without the burden of alcohol to cloud our judgment," Cam reminisced. "We made meals, worked out, watched movies, joked around, talked about the serious side of our marriages that were crumbling," Cam admitted.

"He truly was in my life at the right time, too, Syl. I never want you to think your request for him to stay here was a burden for me. It was the opposite. He saved me from slipping into a funk, feeling sorry for myself after Eleanor left me for another man."

Cam paused and looked up at me. "I have to ask. Are you seeing Nic now?" The question caught me off-guard. I shifted uncomfortably in my chair.

"Uh, well, yes," I admitted thinking how best to describe and classify what kind of relationship Nic and I had.

"He's been very respectful of giving me the space I need to grieve and figure things out on my own. We also have children and don't want to complicate and confuse things unnecessarily for his or my kids right now. When we get a chance to spend time together,

262

it's amazing, but we also need our independence to thrive," I finished, realizing I hadn't entirely clarified what Nic and I had together. Mostly because I didn't really know. I was completely OK not pouring energy into defining that right now.

Cam was quiet as he finished his salad and took a long drink of his raspberry iced tea.

"Well, if the opportunity ever presents itself, I'd love to take you out on a date sometime, Syl." I paused my fork midair to my mouth with my last bite of beet salad, shocked at his proposal.

"I mean it," Cam said. "I've always been attracted to you ever since our college days. I never wanted to admit it because you and Andy were together." I must have been staring blankly at him. "Say something, Syl," Cam said nervously.

"I'm thinking," I said honestly. I couldn't process all of this so quickly. My emotions were all over the board. I didn't want to commit to anything right now. All of a sudden, two lovely men were sending romantic vibes my way.

"Can you give me a little time to think about it, Cam? I truly want to be so careful in each and every move I make in my life. I feel like I'm still in the fog of Andy's death. I want to make sure I make good decisions for me and the kids."

Cam nodded and smiled. "Yeah, that sounds reasonable." He got up to start clearing the dishes back into the house. I helped him wash the dishes inside. Being around Cam was so comfortable. He was kind, considerate, and very attractive to boot.

Cam walked me to my car and I turned to face him, arms outstretched for a hug.

"Thank you," I said as we embraced. "For everything." I stayed in his arms a few moments longer. I knew we both appreciated how good that felt.

When we let go, I kissed him on the cheek. When I stepped back to look at him, he had the biggest smile playing at his lips.

Chapter 49

"I don't even recognize you," Liz, my midwife, commented when she came into the exam room during my annual well woman checkup.

"Same old Syl, rocking a stronger body that supports my life a lot better than my previous body did," I said. I weighed in at 197 having lost close to 100 pounds in the last year. It was crazy to fathom this change. My vitals and blood work were normal and I felt the way I looked; strong and capable, inside and out.

"How are you doing since Andy died, Syl?" Liz turned serious. I wondered if she thought I was starving myself or engaging in disordered eating as a coping mechanism.

"I'm not really sure how I'm supposed to be doing but the kids and I are taking it day by day," I shared.

"We keep having 'firsts' without him. First birthday celebrated without him, first trip to the lakes without him, and soon it will be the first Fourth of July without him," I continued.

"It's so hard to watch the kids navigate as they realize their dad is never going to celebrate another birthday or Christmas with them," I felt myself get sad and Liz didn't seem to want to rush me.

"No more lighting off fireworks on the Fourth of July or trick-or-treating with them. I'm so sad for them, Liz," I sighed and straightened up in my paper gown on the exam table.

"I figure as long as we keep talking about it, and make new memories and traditions, we'll make it through this," I finished. Talking about Andy sometimes made me so down and tired, I had to set limits on how much I let myself talk about my journey.

"Well, Sylvia, it sounds like you have a good handle on this tragedy that struck your family. And you're fit as a fiddle through it all. Is there anything you want to change?" Liz asked me.

"I have you on a low dose antidepressant, do you want to continue that medication?" Liz asked me while reviewing my chart.

"Absolutely, I don't think I'll ever go off that," I admitted. "I function so much better when my brain chemistry is balanced. Along with diet and exercise, I want to respect my mental health especially considering what I put it through over the last year. My kids need me and I need me to be strong in both body and mind."

Liz smiled. "I agree completely. I also think you'd be an incredible coach for others on a path to wellness so if you ever feel like you need a complete change from marketing and sales, healthcare and public health in general needs more people like you!"

"Wow, thank you!" I said excitedly. I hadn't considered that prospect before because I was so tied up with my career at FSG but she was right. I get pretty excited talking about my wellness journey and can see how it fired up others to take charge of their own lives.

I left the appointment feeling like I could take on anything. I was getting the hang of life as a single, working mom. I was grateful for the opportunity to rebuild my life.

Chapter 50

Our first Fourth of July celebration at the lake felt bittersweet. It turned into a large gathering of family and friends. Silas and Katie and the kids were there, Andy's parents came, Roxy and Lin joined in the fun, and I invited Nic and his kids to my parent's house for the day.

All the kids were having such a great time together playing on the beach. Miles and Hannah, Molly and Vinny, and Sammy and Ethan got along famously. They ranged from six to eleven years old which was a perfect blend of ages and stages to get along and play well together.

I was taking it fairly easy and relaxing and visiting. I had competed in my first triathlon the day before. It was an incredible experience. Nic, Roxy, and Lin were there to support me, and I felt confident that I could definitely finish the Half Ironman coming up in September.

I had one more triathlon coming up in August. These building blocks of wins were helping me redefine what my new life looked like. Though many things were out of my control, my health choices, my mindset, and how I treated my family, friends, and career with the respect they deserved were well within my control. I intended to honor these as my guiding principles.

"Is Nic your boyfriend?" Molly asked me as she and Sammy stood in front of Nic and I, dripping wet in their swimsuits. I took my sunglasses off and placed them on my head and looked at Nic, who looked back at me with his eyebrows raised.

"We want to know because we think it would be fun to be sisters," Molly said while Sammy nodded and smiled excitedly next to her. I took a deep breath and realized that all of the adults had stopped what they were doing to look at Nic and I, and wait for the response to Molly's question.

"Yes, he is," I said confidently. Nic reached out and grabbed my hand. I knew these were the words he wanted to hear but he respected me too much to push any labels of a relationship on me too quickly.

"Molly, Nic and I are at the beginning of our relationship, so we're still figuring out how things will work. We're taking things very slowly because I want to honor your dad's memory properly," I continued.

"However, it's really important that you and Sammy stay really good friends because you'll likely be spending a lot more time with one another." I caught Ethan and Vinny high-five each other in the background from the beach. They had paused their game of beach football with one another to listen in as well.

"OK, Mom, that's awesome! I really like Nic!" Molly said, and hugged Nic and almost knocked him over in his chair. Sammy came in close to me, shyly, and whispered, barely audible, "May I hug you?" I scooped her up on my lap and gave her a big hug. Both girls ran back to the beach, back to childhood games and simplicity. I admired their ability to be straight shooters, ask direct questions, and their incredible resilience to adversity.

For the remainder of the afternoon, our family and friends mingled with Nic and I, saying how wonderful it was that we were together. Except Karen and Kenny. I could tell they were hanging back after hearing my announcement about Nic and my relationship.

"Hey, Nic," I said, getting his attention as he'd joined in Ethan and Vinny's beach football game. He stopped and looked up. "Will you please come and formally meet Andy's parents with me?" He grinned at me. "You bet I will."

Nic and I walked over to where Karen and Kenny were sitting with my parents. They were sipping iced tea and watching all their grandkids play.

"Karen and Kenny, I'd like to introduce you to my boyfriend, Nic," Kenny stood up and shook Nic's hand and Karen stood up and shocked me by hugging Nic.

"I'm sorry if we've been a little distant today," Karen said after releasing Nic from her embrace. "We're still moving through the steps of losing our Andy and, well, you seem like a very nice and caring man with both Sylvia and all these kids. Kenny and I are having a tough time hating you," Karen said. The group burst out in laughter at hearing Karen's last line about her and Kenny's plans being foiled about trying to hate Nic.

"I told Karen it wasn't going to work to hate you," Kenny added. "You're too nice of a guy."

"Well, thank you both," Nic said graciously. "Sylvia and her kids are incredible and her family is proving to be exceptional so you better believe I will mind my p's and q's," Nic reassured them.

My parents smiled at Nic. I saw my mom and dad nod at me with their approval. I certainly didn't need their approval, but I can't

271

deny the little girl in me wanted to show her parents she could do a good job. I was relieved they liked Nic.

Roxy and Lin walked up with Silas and Katie, laughing at something.

"I'm getting so much great advice on how to recover and keep myself uninjured for my upcoming races," Roxy gestured toward Silas and Katie. They had been geeking out together over biomechanics, injury prevention, and a myriad of other training and recovery techniques athletes use to perform optimally.

"Take me out on your boat so the lake noise will drown out their voices," Lin insisted. "They won't stop talking about exercise!"

My dad hopped up and headed down to the beach to let the kids know they could go tubing behind the boat. All six kids let out happy whoops and hollers.

Chapter 51

We spent the rest of the afternoon soaking up the sun and good conversation and laughs with one another. We enjoyed amazing grilled foods. The kids took turns going tubing until their arms were so sore they couldn't hold on to the handles anymore.

At the end of the day, I asked my dad if Nic and I could take the pontoon out for a sunset cruise with our kids before they headed back to Fargo.

"Sylvia, why don't they just stay?" My dad insisted. "The kids are having such a great time together. They shouldn't have to miss the fireworks and I don't want them to drive home after that! We have enough room. The kids can sleep on air mattresses and you two can have the guest bedroom in the basement."

I said goodbye to Roxy and Lin, who were headed back to Fargo, and Karen and Kenny, who had to drive back to the farm in Dooley. Katie and Silas were taking their kids to watch the fireworks in town from the city beach.

Nic and I loaded all four kids into the pontoon. They were layered in a coating of bug spray and in their life jackets over jammies. We brought blankets and sweatshirts to wrap up in if they got cold after sunset. We also grabbed a few pairs of noise-canceling headphones in case the fireworks show over the lake became too loud or scary for the kids.

We trolled around the lake as the sun slowly set in the west, quiet as we reveled in the sounds of the kids playing and talking with each other, the beginning booms of fireworks in the distance. I smiled at Nic and I could tell he was pleased with the direction our relationship was going. Plus, my dad had given him the keys to operate the pontoon so I think he was puffed up with pride to take on the role of captain.

The fireworks began at dusk, a little after 10 PM, and Nic cut the motor and anchored down. He cuddled with me under my cozy fleece blanket. The kids' talking ceased. They laid on their backs and took in the lit-up sky with an occasional "Oooh" and "Ahhh" when they saw something particularly spectacular.

When the show ended, all of us clapped in appreciation. Nic brought up the anchor and motored us back home to my parents' place. By the time Nic docked the boat in the lift, the girls had fallen asleep.

Nic and I carefully took off their lifejackets and carried each of our daughters up the stairs and into the house and laid them gently next to one another on an air mattress. Ethan and Vinny followed quietly behind us and collapsed on an air mattress right next to where Molly and Sammy slept. There was a third mattress that held Hannah and Miles.

My heart was filled with so much love to see all these tuckered out kids slumbering.

Nic and I made our way to the guest bedroom, falling into bed exhausted and content after a fulfilling day. As we settled in, Nic as the big spoon, and me as the little spoon, Nic whispered into my ear, "I love you, Sylvia Wilde. Thank you for being my girlfriend. I will do my best to be the best boyfriend I can be."

I rolled over to face him and kissed him slowly and deeply.

"I love you, too, Dominic Bennett. You are my greatest surprise that I would have never imagined could come out of something so tragic in my life. I'm excited for what the future holds for us. Goodnight, darling."

Sneak Peak of Book Two in the Disruptress Series

REFORMED

I dipped my toe in the chilly water as the sun was rising and steam rose off the lake. I swung my arms to stay loose, warm, and shake off nerves ahead of the start of the Wildlife Loop Triathlon in Custer, South Dakota. I visualized two laps around Stockade Lake to account for 1.2 miles of swimming. That was only the beginning as I was slated to complete 56 miles of cycling through Custer State Park (I was hopeful for some buffalo sightings along the way), followed by a half marathon to finish off my multi-sport feat.

"You got this, Syl!" I turned to see Nic smiling and giving me two thumbs up. He was flanked on both sides by our kids and my parents. Andy's parents were there as well standing next to Lin, Roxy's wife. I gave a smile and wave back to my tribe.

"How do you feel?" Roxy grabbed my hand tightly as she stood in knee-deep water next to me. She'd completed several full Ironman distance triathlons yet she was accompanying me on my first half Ironman distance.

"I feel really good, Rox," I said. "A little nervous. I want to get started already," I added impatiently.

Our entire family, along with Roxy and Lin, was staying at a seven bedroom cabin at a resort nearby for the long Labor Day weekend and I had been up since 4 AM fueling and preparing for the long athletic day ahead. I knew starting the race would help me settle my nerves. Instead of all the thinking and preparing, I could focus on letting my body take over and do what I had trained it to do.

The race director raised the megaphone and rattled off last minute instructions for water safety and transition area rules and then raised his air horn to signal the start. We were off.

"This one's for you, Andy," I said quietly as I plunged my face into the water and began rhythmically swimming the freestyle.

REFORMED available Spring 2020.

Made in the USA
Monee, IL
04 January 2024

51088723R00162